Frank James Mathew

A Child in the Temple

A novel

Frank James Mathew

A Child in the Temple
A novel

ISBN/EAN: 9783337049027

Printed in Europe, USA, Canada, Australia, Japan

Cover: Foto ©Andreas Hilbeck / pixelio.de

More available books at **www.hansebooks.com**

A Child in the Temple

BY

FRANK MATHEW, 1865 - 1924

JOHN LANE: THE BODLEY HEAD
LONDON AND NEW YORK
1897

CB

University Press:

JOHN WILSON AND SON, CAMBRIDGE, U.S.A.

Contents

A Child in the Temple

PROLOGUE

HOW THE CARRIAGE CAME TO KILMORNA

AS I sit here in my quiet room in the Temple, it seems to me now it is always morning in Ireland; for the tints of the moors and woods remain as keen as they were in the prime of the day, and the early freshness is there till the dusk begins to blacken the mountains. Or does my memory trip, as I go back to the time when it was morning with me? I hope some trace of that time will be with me yet, when the dusty afternoon wanes and is forgotten in twilight.

I   I

A Child in the Temple

These things happened in London yesterday, yet as I am going to write them, my
memory is first on the years when I was a
child at Kilmorna, — a house in a woody nook
of the hills. I can see now it was forlorn
and forsaken ; but it was pleasant to me, as I
ran wild in the tangled park, or among the
creepers entwined across the ways in the
garden, where grass grew on the paths and
ivy over the walls. The house was one
storey high, and my people had added a
wing here and there, as the fancy took them,
and so it sprawled with dim galleries and
wainscotted rooms looking out on long grass
and leafy bushes of lilac.

Just as I took pleasure in prowling in the
desolate places, so I also enjoyed things sore
to Aunt Elizabeth, such as the attention of
moonlighters. Because my uncle was poor,

Kilmorna

he had to press for the rents, and so the moonlighters wasted powder behind hedges and walls if he drove out after dark, and they employed part of their habitual leisure in writing him messages with drawings of skulls, and would come in the night and dig a grave by the steps. Uncle Andrew did not mind them at all, till they took to digging the graves; but that annoyed him because he had to heed where he went, and it was his custom to moon happily with a look of despair. The only time I ever saw him put out was when he had gone for a stroll in a shower and had tumbled into a grave; and then he said he was reluctant to spoil any one's amusements, but thought the tenants were unkindly considerate.

That morning, he gave way to my aunt's long eagerness for a guard of policemen; and after that, if he went out for a drive, a couple of constables would sit in the back of the dog-cart with rifles, and if he strolled in the park, they would follow, a little distance behind. Often, I saw him slouching along the weedy paths with his hands thrust in the pockets of his wrinkled grey coat, or at rest on a fallen tree in the grounds, or kneeling to look close at a beetle or an ant, while all the time it was plain he had forgotten his escort, till seeing them, he started abashed, and came again to the house with an attempt to be busy. Afraid he could not dismiss the constables without hurting their feelings, he began to stop in, or would try to slip out when there was nobody looking, while the police were at dinner; and at other times he would peer from a window, as if the house was a prison.

Kilmorna

My aunt was a delicate little woman, with white hair and a cold regular face, and a distant manner, though sometimes, when she was talking to friends, there was a tremulous sweetness about her eyes and her lips. As I remember her first, she was severe with the peasants, though she came of a house that had befriended the people. But all was going wrong with her then; for the estate was encumbered, and the creditors hard, and her only son was away. Besides, she was getting old, and her heart had gone away with her son. Even in her unhappiest time, she was always tender to me.

The cares of the house fell on her, for my uncle had let her do as she chose with it, while he was with snails. When darkness filled the house, I would carry a light, as she let the constables in. Being very small, I would hold the lantern over my head, and it would flash on the periwigged portraits in the galleries, and their faces would look so aghast as they peeped out of the blackness that they would frighten us both, and her bony and little hand would clutch mine till I was hurt by her rings. Small wonder if those forgotten Kilmornas started aghast at this outcome of their irrational life! In her left hand, she would have a rusty and ruinous pistol of old duelling times; but she was always afraid it had been loaded by accident. When we got to the door, she would open it a bit, keeping the chain fastened, and cry, "Who is there?" and the constables would answer, "Police." "Are you sure you're the police?" she would ask, for fear it was a trick of the moonlighters.

The constables were my heroes, of course,

and I would pester them, and was never so happy as when I shouldered a rifle, and attempted to fasten a helmet on the back of my head so that the brim would not come over my face. I made up my mind to be a constable too, when I was big; but Curly's only ambition was to be masked and lurk about as a moonlighter. From her tenderest years, Curly had an affection for crime. When we were not racing our ponies, or roasting potatoes in the garden, or making believe to be squirrels as we climbed in the trees, our favourite game was one we called "moonlighting," — at least it was hers; though as I was the landlord and had nothing to do but to fall, I used to find it monotonous, but pretended to like it, for Curly Adair had all the love of my heart.

Adair was over the hills, a dozen miles

A Child in the Temple

from Kilmorna; but Curly stayed with us
often, and though I was a little older, would
govern me, as a matter of course. Soon after
we met, she informed me she was going to
marry me when I was a constable, if I proved
to be tall enough. I had no fear about that,
as I intended to be six foot at the least, and
have a moustache as big as Sergeant Molloy's; and so the matter was settled. After
that, when we had tea in the doll's cups, we
would make believe to be married, and so sit
silent and glum, as if we had nothing to say.
But that was a trial to her, for she was always
a chatterbox, and so she would break in, of
a sudden, with "Whisper, Larry," forgetting
the solemn rules of the game. "Whisper,
Larry," was her commonest phrase, when
something came to her mind; and just now
as I wrote it, I seemed to hear it again in

8

that adorable brogue, and to see a blithe little woman with strong haunting blue eyes and gilt brown curls, and the shortest of frocks, and the proudest of airs if grown-up people were looking; though she was wild and full of masterful fun when we were playing together.

Though I answered to " Larry," I had been cruelly christened Florence, because it was a family name and the Kilmornas had borne it till my grandfather died. Most of them proved riotous and redoubtable Florences. Florence the Hare, the fifth earl, and his son, Florence the Cask, and Florence of the Guns, are remembered and admired for their sins; but I looked down on them all for not disowning the name. I had a particular grudge against the man who put up the battered arch in the garden, with that mossy irregular inscription to say it had been erected by Florence, first Earl of Kilmorna, in 1610. So I christened myself Lawrence, and refused to submit to the indignity of the name of a girl.

The only thing I envied my uncle was his name, though the people had altered it to "Andy the Owl." Though I was fond of him in a pitying way, I used to blush for his old clothes and his moonstruck moping appearance, when he took me for a walk through the village, and went slouching along with his soft hat on the back of his head, and glowering through his glasses, and stumbling over the children and the pigs on the path. Sometimes he stumbled over me, if he met me in the park or the house, — and that I could not forgive. Still, he was gentle and good to me, so I had a fatherly tenderness for his failings and ugliness. But I used to wonder my aunt was not stern with him, for she let him go on just as he liked, and only interfered when she asked him to come to church of a Sunday, from time to time; and then I was wretched, for he would keep dropping his book, and turning round in the pew to stare at the neighbours, as if he thought they were beetles, or would collapse limp in an attitude of studied ungainliness, and gape at the rector with such despairing astonishment that the poor fellow would falter and break down in his sermon. Yet my uncle and aunt understood one another perfectly, so Curly and I said they must have talked a deal once, for now they never opened their lips.

We considered my uncle selfish, as he had boxes and drawers full of old beetles he

A Child in the Temple

would not lend us to play with. It was not
as if he had been fond of them, for those
beetles were dead. If they had been alive in
the boxes, of course it would have been a
different thing. Often, Curly would not let
me come near her white rat, or the frog she
used to carry about in a chocolate-box; but
that was not selfishness, for they might not
have liked it. Besides, she was very generous with them at times, and once put the
white rat in my aunt's bed of a morning, as
a pleasant surprise. But, as Curly said
afterwards, old people are strange, and you
never can tell what they will really like.
Now, there was that moonlighting game of
ours, — it was capital fun, but my aunt could
not abide it; and I believe that was because
Curly added a war-whoop and a tomahawk
to it, while the only part I enjoyed was the

chance of giving a shriek when I was shot
by the pea-gun.   Moonlighters were wonderful beings to us: and we never connected
them with the doleful indifferent peasants we
saw at work in the fields, or sitting smoking
on walls, or leading donkeys with burdens
of turf by the grassy and shady road to the
village.

Because we were told to keep away from
the tenants, we used to go, on the sly, to
their farms, and had a welcome from all.
We told them we meant to run away and be
married; and this appeared to excite them,
and they wished us a number of children, and
said it would be a happy time for the poor
when we lived up at the House.   I daresay
some of our hosts could ill spare the stir-
about; or the milk they provided, but nothing was grudged; and I remember one of the

poorest insisted on giving Curly a kid we fastened in a nook of the park and cherished there till my uncle tumbled over it once when he was chasing a beetle.

The farm we liked best was Moroney's, a prosperous snug house on a hill; for two girls of our own ages were there, and used to treat us with reverence. Kitty Moroney was full of life, though her sister Molly was quiet; and we got on so well with them that Curly intended to have them as bridesmaids in spite of their humble birth, and we let them into the secret when we made up our minds to run away for the wedding. But when that fateful morning arrived, and we started to walk to Dublin, several hundreds of miles off, the little Moroneys could not get out of school, and the rain came on, and Curly tumbled into a wayside ditch as she showed me how far she was not able to jump, and so she called me a beast, and we quarrelled all the way home.

When Curly was away, I went round with my aunt to protect her; and for most my sixth winter we were seldom apart, as Uncle Andrew was ailing and remained in his room. So I could sit in his big chair by the fire of an evening, while Aunt Elizabeth worked and kept on telling me things of days when she was a girl, or more remarkable legends: the country stories of ghosts came pat to her tongue, and she believed in them all. I would listen to her, till my heart was in sympathy with the quivering of the lace on her wrists and of the light on her rings. Her stiff way and prim accent would have been enough to convince a more in-

A Child in the Temple

credulous mind: and I could but share her belief, though I knew it would be manly to doubt.

Most of all, she would dwell on unhappy legends of warnings; for her people had a banshee, whose lament was heard in the dark when one was going to die. When she sat up with her dying father, she heard the wailing herself, for it rang through the Castle three times, like the clamouring of a terrible wind, and yet the weather was still. But when the Kilmornas were dying, a ghostly carriage would come to take the soul on its journey. As the watchers were praying beside the bed, they would hear the wheels on the avenue, and then on the gravel beside the steps at the door. Then there would be a ring at the bell, and the soul would go away on its wandering.

These legends clutched me, till I would often be wakeful and think the rush of the wind under the old trees on the avenue was the clatter of wheels. Then I would hold my breath, and my ears would seem to grow till I thought they would be as big as a rabbit's; and sometimes I would leap out of my bed, and run to the window to see the shadowy carriage — with its dim lights like far-off will-o'-the-wisps, and the cloudy forms of its headless coachman and its horses — arrive with that irresistible summons. My uncle was so ill that the carriage might come for him any night; and, in ignorance of the meaning of death, I used to wish he would die, to let me see it for once. But I saw the menacing trees, and heard the groans of the branches, and the cries of the wind.

If my aunt noticed my fear, she would

A Child in the Temple

break off, and begin to talk of that other subject of hers, — her big adventurous son. I was to do my best to grow up to be like him, she said; but it occurs to me now there were some of his ways she had not fully considered. But then, there is no knowing what things a good woman will love if they are done by her boy. As far as I could understand, he was taller than any one, and spent most his time thrashing men bigger, or making fierce love to all the girls in the county, — and I was quite willing to do the same, in my turn. My cousin, Terence, had gone to make his fortune in diggings at the other end of the world; and when he came back, the shining days would begin: for he would pay the mortgages off, and then put everything right, since she took it for granted he would be rolling in money, as he used to say he would be. But whether or no, she wearied now for him always, and only wanted him back.

"When Terence is back," was often too on my uncle's lips, when I was with him; for now, because he was bedridden, I liked to sit by his side, in the musty and darkened room, with a feeling of responsible strength, since I found myself taking care of a man.

"Terence will see to that, when he comes," he would say, if anything worried him; or, "Has the post come? Then why has nobody gone for it? Go and tell John to ride at once to the village," — forgetting the only servants we had were a couple of women to wait on us, and to tidy the few rooms we kept open, for most the house was shut up, in those evil days of our poverty.

That was a wild winter: the days were

A Child in the Temple

bitter and dark, and the wind was dreadful at night. My Aunt Elizabeth grew more silent, and seemed to notice me less, and was so seldom away from the sick-room, that I began to believe she was fond of my uncle: and this surprised me, since Curly and I had decided grown-up people grew tired of one another as soon as they had been married a little, for we were cynical in the pauses of games, though our doubts were only put on in an attempt to be wise.

Christmas Eve came in with a storm; and the wind yelled in the corridors, as we sat by the fire. Uncle Andrew was worse, and a servant was sitting up with him, while we tried in vain to get warm. Long watching had told on my aunt; and she was white and despairing, and started at every shriek of the

wind. The lantern was ready; and we sat
waiting to let the constables in. With a
hard face, she bent over some work, and her
lips moved as they did in church, and once
she whispered, "He can't be taken; I have
borne enough;" and another time she cried
out, "Oh! what is that?" when it was only
the storm.

"The wind, auntie," said I.

"Thank God!" she said, and I wondered,
and then saw she had feared it was the banshee; and my heart leapt with hope, for
though I would rather have watched the
ghostly carriage arriving, it would be something to listen to that wail, and so at once I
went off in a dream of describing the whole
occurrence to Curly. In those days the
things that happened to me were only of
interest because I could describe them to

A Child in the Temple

Curly: and all I did was intended to win the crown of her praise. But soon my aunt's fears gained on me, and I started whenever the wind rose, or a door slammed in the passage; but still I had no share in her sorrow, and in the lulls of the gale I stared at the red turf, and kept wondering what presents would be put in my stockings and attempting to forget a misgiving there would be nothing at all. I chiefly wanted a pony-chaise, a rifle, a musical-box, and a gold-headed cane. As I debated whether I had much prospect of getting a drum into the bargain, or one of those boxes of beetles, since Uncle Andrew never played with them now, and would not want them again, there was a shriek, by the window, that seemed louder than any noise I had heard, and it froze me; and Aunt Elizabeth sprang to her feet, putting her hands up to her face, as she cried out, "The banshee!"

As that wail shook us again, there was a rush in the dark, and I leapt up crying, "The carriage!" Aunt Elizabeth caught my left hand, and hurried into the passage: it was all I could do to keep up with her, and the corridor echoed with cries, and things were shoving me back, and white and peri-wigged faces glimmered aghast along the sides of the wall.

As we reached the mat, that wail deafened me for some moments, and then I heard the wheels on the avenue. My heart was ice at that sound: and I tried to tug my aunt back, as she was pulling the rusty and thick bolt of the door.

"Don't open it, auntie," I cried, as she unfastened the chain and turned the key, and the wind swooped on the door and struck it instantly open. I reeled back, and the lantern fell, with a clatter of broken glass, on the ground. She staggered too; and I clutched her, for I was crazy with terror.

There, in the wild darkness, the carriage was coming headlong towards us. I saw it plainly, and the shadowy driver, and the horses, and the couple of lights. It dashed up to the door, and the lights blinded me, as Aunt Elizabeth sprang forward, as if she was thrusting somebody back.

"You sha'n't take him!" she cried. "He is all I have in the world. In God's name, take me instead!"

A black figure leapt from the dim carriage, and sprang towards her in silence. I shrieked, and flung myself in front of her, crying, "You must n't touch her!" But I was tumbled aside.

"Mother dear!" cried her son, clasping her very tight in his arms.

CHAPTER I

A HERMIT IN LONDON

SHADOWS and dust are in the rooms of Kilmorna: and my people are gone. The fifteen years since that stormy Christmas have left the house like a tomb, and the pleasant garden a tangle. Yet they had brought happiness there; for when my cousin came back in that dreaded carriage, our troubles were ended by the fortune he found in the mines: and so my uncle took heart, and making friends with his tenants, and getting rid of the constables with extravagant fees and praises, was as lively as ever — though that is not saying much — and went

26

off hunting the snails. It took Aunt Elizabeth days to get over her dread that the whole affair was a dream, as she sat gloating on Terence and did not open her lips. Most were silent with him, for the man was an irrepressible talker, and had plenty to tell of his adventurous freaks.

Every one appeared to think Terence was master: and I valued his kindness more than my aunt's love, and obeyed him humbly, though the slightest reproof from her would make me indignant. I had an affectionate scorn of her age and my uncle's misty and deplorable manner; but my cousin was faultless. Even on the day when, inspired by an unusual devil, I had thrown Curly's shoe in the pond, to see if it would float, I was not angry, though just as I was whooping and laughing in triumph, as she stood on one leg in a frenzy, he came up at my back, and before I knew he was there, I was flying through space and sousing into the water. "I wanted to see if you would float," he remarked, as I scrambled forth; and I considered him right, though Curly condoled with me and could not forgive him.

That is all over now, and here I sit in the Temple. It is Christmas Day, and the snow is sheeting the miles of roofs I can see from my room at the top of this old rickety house, and the sun has come out, and the bells all over London are chiming. I have set to work to write out the story of yesterday's remarkable things, before their remembrance has any time to be dulled. If I have told of Kilmorna, it is because yesterday's doings are children of that prologue of life before my exile began.

A Hermit in London

When it was dusk yesterday, I stood at my window, and looked down at the white gardens, and the shadowy river beyond, and the red domes of the light under the black arches of Waterloo Bridge, and the dark hulk of Westminster jutting before a sunset that flared like a wild and menacing dawn. The snow was lending judicial ermine to the trees in the Temple, and heavy wigs to the roofs.

It seemed so chill out of doors that I turned away with a shiver, and poked my fire till it was flushing my books with a kinder glow than the sunset's, and I was heartened by that; and Mab, the most sympathetic and friendly little dog in the world, was cheered also, and had a mind for a romp, and so hung on to my trousers with such a resolute bite that she was hauled

A Child in the Temple

along the floor as I moved, — and at this she pretended to be very indignant, and growled savagely, though at times her hilarity grew so wild that she was forced to rush round the room, but did it silently; for because she has spent the only year of her life with me, she knows it is wrong to bark in the Temple, though I never told her indeed, but she has noticed my quietness, as she shares my heart-heaviness if by chance I am glum, and thus has grown so discreet that she has the name of an inarticulate terrier.

Then I sat down on my deck chair by the hearth, and Mab jumped on my knee, and so we stared at the flames, as if our minds were together. Since I bought her as a very small pup, we have been seldom asunder. Mostly, at that time of the day, we go for strolls on the windy Embankment and round the Green

A Hermit in London

Park, for I keep my room till the twilight makes reading bad for my eyes: I lead her chained, for she is eager to welcome any stranger with love, and so might follow a thief. In the evenings, she takes a nap on my knees, with her head snug on the crook of my left arm, as I hold a volume up to the light, while my other hand turns the pages, or strokes her intellectual head, or pulls her tail when I want her to express her approval. Then every night, I dress her up in an old flannel tennis-shirt, and, wrapping her snugly in her particular blanket, let her sleep in the corner of my bed; for the only time I attempted to persuade her to have a nook of her own in a big box, she kept trotting about the room, in the dark, with such heartbroken whimpering — as if she believed she was abandoned for ever — that I was forced to get up and put her by me again.

A Child in the Temple

Her only fault is a weakness for worrying papers, and I had to be careful not to let any fall, till I trained her to carry them down to the porter's lodge in the basement — if I was out of the room — instead of eating them, and so they were saved. This succeeded so well that I then taught her to take letters down when I wanted them posted, and messages expressing her needs; and the only time this had failed was when I gave her a card with "Please give Mab a bath" on it, and as she loathes being washed, she ate it up, on the way.

These rooms are under the roof of number Five, Plowden Buildings — on the right of Middle Temple Lane, as you go down to the River; and if you should be passing this way, you have only to step into the black hall, where you will see columns of names on either side, and then you can come up the dim stairs; and if you are hardy and active, and so get to the top, you can find " Mr. Fenton " in white letters above the dingy door on the left, and knock at it, and annoy him extremely.

The chambers next mine belong to Foster, my only friend in the house; for though it is teeming with fellows, I hardly know them by sight. I have three rooms; and this one is sombre with wainscot and books, and it is dark from old fires, and I like to think Goldsmith, my hero, may have been in it once. My rooms are tidied by old Mrs. Maclean, — a meek motherly woman, who spends most her time soothing her big husband, a tottering and implacable fighter. They have a son, a dark and bearded policeman, with a philosopher's eyes. This son, John Peter, has tried a number of trades and come to grief in them

A Child in the Temple

all, because Nature jocosely made him a gentleman, unable to cringe, and forgot to give him a mind. Last Christmas, his father and he came up to my rooms, uninvited, in kilts, and strode round playing the pipes, till they cured my old wish to go to visit the Highlands. The old man and his wife are full of zeal; and I value their service the more, as the neighbouring houses depend on the short care of dilapidated laundresses who live in the slums.

My meals are sent in from Dick's Coffee-house, and so I can live as secluded here as I like, as so many thousands have done, in the hushed squares and narrow streets of the Temple. Though of course I know many in London, I am nothing to them; and so they are as little to me as people I pass when I lead Mab along the misty Embankment.

A Hermit in London

Here I am addicted to dreams nobody
would have ever suspected. I am reluctant
to write it, still I may as well get it over, —
though I am now twenty-one, and thus un-
likely to grow, I seldom come on a man as
small and slight as myself, and if I do, I de-
spise him. To make it worse, nature afflicts
me with a boyish and round face, and light
curls, and a wistful and inquisitive look that
drives me to frenzy if I catch a glimpse of
myself as I am passing a mirror. Before I
bought Mab, I used to try to keep scowling
with squeezed lips, as I read, in the hope
of acquiring a stern and resolute air; but
she cured me of that, by gazing at me in
breathless alarm, as if she thought I was
ill.

This girlish appearance of mine has no
effect on my dreams; for they are full of ad-

A Child in the Temple

ventures. As I sit in my long chair, of an evening, it suddenly shifts from my dusky room to a plunging deck, and I am off on my wandering, where the wind goes. Or at other times I am bearded and big, and as I gallop through wilds, with a rifle slung at my back and a brace of revolvers stuck in my belt, I have a red shirt, and my riding-boots are near to my waist. But the strange thing is that I am never alone; for some one is there galloping also, or walks the deck at my side, when the ship is standing out and the morning is soaring up from the sea.

That comrade of my dreams is a masterful girl, who has won renown as a rider over rickety walls and rushy moors in the West. Some people say she has never read a book in her life; but that is not so, for I saw her study her catechism. True, that was a long

time ago, when we were young at Kilmorna.
Now her gilt curls are quelled, and she has
certainly grown silent; but that suits me, because I have a weakness for talking, as Mab
knows, when she listens for hours to my
chatter, and joins in it with her answering tail.
Curly is so tall that her height would have
been suited to mine, if I could have managed
to grow, and she is comely to see; and her
face and her eyes are just as fresh as the
morning. The last time I had seen her was
a couple of years ago, when I was over in
Ireland, and then only the fact I was poor
prevented my proposing; and yet as I watched
her riding a cantankerous brute, I reflected she
would master me soon; but I said to myself,
my wife would be certain to rule me, and I
would rather be bullied by a big girl than by
a little one, anyway. No more rides in the

A Child in the Temple

wind for stately Curly Adair. I might dream of her as much as I liked, while she was shut in by convent walls as a nun.

Curly is in London to-day, for she came over to work as a Sister at Jerusalem House. Every one knows the " Little Sisters," and the look of the carts they drive round, as they beg from friends or gather food for the old people and the children they shelter. I have been more than once to the convent, to see after Irish people, and I have a deal of respect for the Sisters, though I think them too kind; for most the old folk are ungrateful, and appear to have learnt daintiness in lives in the slums. One time I was visiting, all the old men were threatening to go on a strike in a body, and said unless they were given a dryer brand of champagne with their lunch, or some other improvement, — I forget what it was, —

they would march right out of the house,
and lie down in the nearest gutter, and
starve; so the poor nuns were simply wild
with despair.

But I had taken good care to keep away
from the convent after Curly had come.
While she lived as a nun, how could she be
more than the ghost of the eager girl I remembered? I still thought of her riding against
a blustering wind, across the moors by the
sea. When my friends die, I keep apart from
their places, and half believe they are there
and remember me still and I shall see them
again. I have moods when I think my uncle
and aunt are still beyond at Kilmorna, passing their days peacefully in silent companion-
ship; and yet it is years since they died:
and as I lounged in my chair yesterday, I
was heavy at heart to think my cousin had

followed them, — poor Terence, **the** kindest
and most immoral of men.

When Uncle Andrew died, Terence succeeded to the title, and came to London, and
was known as the mad Lord Kilmorna, for
his doings were hardly fit for our respectable days. If he had lived in old times, and
thrashed watchmen, or hunted the citizens
through Piccadilly at night, he would have
astonished none but his unfortunate victims.
Now he was not able to drive in the Row,
or have a turn on the River in his launch,
the "Iniquity," without being summoned,
and would have passed most of his nights in
a lock-up, but the policemen were tired of
spending weeks in the hospital, and let him
alone. Sometimes they had revenge on his
friends, and only a month ago took up Foster

A Hermit in London

instead, when in a moment of lofty emotion he was led to declaim, "Give me liberty, or give me death!" while a dozen or so of them were assisting the porters to tempt Terence away from the Criterion at midnight. Well, to cut a long story short, Terence lived for nothing but wine, women, and song, and was so big and good-looking and full of irrational happiness, that even his only enemies, the police, could not bear him a grudge; and when he died, he was sincerely regretted by an army of friends and a large circle of creditors.

Yesterday I was thinking about him, and wondered what would become of his property; for though more than a week had passed since I had heard of his being washed overboard, when he was out in his yacht on that sunny and wild morning, his affairs were unknown. Foster had hinted Caterina

A Child in the Temple

Moroni would take it under a will; but still I hoped for the House, since it would be dull to be twelfth Earl of Kilmorna and as poor as the dead.

The entail had been cut off, and the place had been Terence's to treat as he liked; but I have always a knack of trusting my hopes, and this made me sure he must have left me Kilmorna, since he had plenty of money to give to any one else, — for only an inherited hatred of paying debts had prevented his making creditors happy. Caterina Moroni would probably have a share of his cash, — she had found her way to the stage through him, for he had heard her at home. In those days she was Kitty Moroney of the Farm on the Hill. But he had been in love with so many girls that he had not heeded her much till her success in the summer;

though since then he had moved heaven and earth to be allowed to protect her from the dangers of London.

I had a weakness for Kitty too, as I think most of us had; for it was hard to resist her winning laugh, and her wheedling soothering brogue, and those clear eyes that every man in the theatre fancied had dwelt on him with a particular kindness. When she sprang on the stage at the Gaiety, the theatre thrilled. Callous and callow youths of fashion forgot their frigid bearing, and shouted, and as for Terence, he was so carried away by enthusiasm that he could hardly refrain from assaulting all the men within reach, — and indeed one time his sheer happiness led him to bring down such a blow on the young Duke of Lincoln's bald head that the disturbance was frightful.

A Child in the Temple

As a rule, I go seldom to the theatres; for though I enjoy them, I am as happy at home, so why should I turn out in the cold, at the risk of finding a piece stupid, when I have plenty of books? But I shudder to think of what I squandered on stalls at the Gaiety, though I considered myself deeply in love with Curly Adair, and she had nothing in common with dainty and dark Kitty Moroney, of the mocking amorous ways and the irresistible laugh.

Foster promised to let me meet Kitty, and could have done it with ease, for his shaven and narrow face and long legs and frozen look are familiar at the back of the scenes on all the stages in town. I made his acquaintance one night, when he was attempting to open my door in the belief it was his: he was calm at the time and dignified, but

hardly intelligent. Next morning, he saun-
tered into my room as if he had known me
for years, and since then he has shared all
my belongings. To do him justice, he is
ready to share his small possessions with
me, but as a rule he is penniless; and when
he is not, it would never occur to me to
plunder his rooms. And he is generous,
too, for more than once he has given me an
extravagant dinner with money I lent him to
keep his creditors quiet. "Come, let us
drink, forgetful of that imminent wolf," he
exclaims, till all the money is gone.

Apparently he has many relations, for I
often see girls on the landing, and he says
they are cousins. A love of music and noise
appears to run in the family. But for all
his gay life, he is not seldom dependent on
the store of sardines and biscuits and Chianti

A Child in the Temple

I keep in a deed-box, with "Kilmorna Estate" on it. Before I got Mab, I used to dine on them, when the weather was such I had not the heart to send Maclean out in it with a message for "Dick's." But since she has controlled me, I dine on cutlets all the year round; because they provide her with satisfactory bones. I feel I have to make up to her for her slavery here; and I am full of remorse when she is clanking her chain, — a little innocent convict. I dream of watching her scamper about the lawns of my home, when my weary exile is over. Lord! how glad she will be when she has freedom at last, and how fierce she will try to look, as she chases the scudding leaves and the rabbits and the birds of the air — not wanting to hurt them, but only for the fun of the thing!

A Hermit in London

So I thought yesterday, and taking hold
of her right paw, I shook it, to show I had
her in mind, because I know she is sensitive. At this she made believe to devour
my hand, as she had nothing to say. My
heart was sore for a sight of the kindly faces
at home. For that was one of the times
when my fancies have a quieter haunt, and
I find myself wishing to earn my bread as a
gardener in some ivied old house, where, in
place of drafting the writs, I should be
grafting the roses, and, no longer bustling
about the quarrelsome Courts, I should strip
the green insects from the plants, with apol-
ogies for disturbing them, and drop the snails
tenderly into the grounds of the neighbours.
For I have a liking for flowers, though to
keep them cut, in a room, seems to me like
nursing a friend ailing of an incurable ill-

A Child in the Temple

ness. So might my name be inherited, without risk of dishonour, by innocent generations of roses.

Yet at other times I will handle my revolver, and dream of firing at some one, or pressing it to an enemy's forehead. I bought a revolver last birthday, — for I give myself presents, as nobody else remembers the date, — and since then I have always carried it, hoping for an occasion to use it; though I only load it with blank cartridges, — for I would not like to hurt any one, any more than would Mab. It was wonderful how manly I felt when I had that weapon at last. Like Terence, I should have lived in old times, and had a weapon to wear. A periwig would have given my face a stronger look: and high heels would have been just what I wanted. I would have swaggered terribly with the longest of swords, — as Goldsmith did, when they called him a fly stuck on a pin, — and a bloom-coloured coat would have been extremely becoming.

Even in the drab clothes of our time, the revolver's weight in my pocket was enough to make me feel big: and I remember I went into the club, and saw Foster there with his back to me, and I heard him say, "Baby Bunting is a kind little fool, though he is always meddling and prattling; but I hardly trust him, because he is too good to be true." Then he broke off as he saw me; so for a moment I fancied he was talking of me, and I nearly pulled out my revolver, to show him I was not such a child as I looked; but then I felt I was wrong. Said I to him afterwards, "Who's that fellow Bunting you spoke about?" But he did not reply.

A Child in the Temple

Well, yesterday, as the glow of the fire strengthened in the twilight, I wandered to the places of home.

It was a morning on the brink of the summer, and Curly and I were standing out on the steps, as the men brought the horses round from the stables, and Mab was off in the meadows, hunting a lark that twinkled against the sky like a brown star quiring to young-eyed cherubim, and the hawthorn was blowing, and the scythes hissed on the wet lawns by the lilac, with the sound of smooth waves on a sandy shore, and a haze like the bloom of a peach was on the light of the woods.

Then the fire sank for a time, and the scene changed of a sudden.

It was a brown evening in autumn, and the air was good with the smell of damp earth and wet trees, as we were riding home under

branches, in a lane where a calf, with big
ears and an astounded expression, was looking across the ferns on a wall, while Mab was
trotting beside us, with the virtuous air of a
little dog that has run several miles, and so
has too much sense to be fooling with rust-
ling frolicking leaves, and right in front of
us smoked the thatched roofs of the village:
and as the surly grunting of sows, and the
hysterical conversation of hens, and the
homely smell of the peat, and the caterwaul-
ing and the sobs of a donkey, reached us
faintly, the place was like a long farm; while
the folk were out by their doors, discussing
the day's excitements, the birth of several
pigs in Rooney's family circle, and the deeds
of Mulligan's mare; and I knew every one
of them would brighten with friendliness as
they saw us go by.

A Child in the Temple

Then as a knock at the door summoned me from my dreams, I got up, but little thought I was going to find use for my revolver at last, and come across Kitty Moroney and even Curly Adair.

CHAPTER II

SOME GUESTS IN THE TEMPLE

A MAN once was three days climbing a mountain, and came down in two minutes. The work of my dreams was ruinous as suddenly now; for as I opened the door, there was a wind of disaster. Was it the draught, or a foreboding of loans?

"Cigarettes?" Foster said, as he came into the room.

"Here," said I, meekly, as I sank in my chair and snapped my fingers for Mab. But she would have snapped her fingers at me, if her paws had been hands; for when a stranger is by, she does not trouble to notice me. I try to persuade myself only her ideas of Irish hospitality move her, but I am secretly jealous.

"How snug you are here!" said Foster, as he was filling his case; and this depressed me, for he always pretends to envy my comfort when he is going to lessen it.

"So, so," I replied.

"Do you know how lucky you are?" said he, impressively. "That title of yours—"

"Don't talk of that!" I said gloomily.

"It might have been English."

"Well, yes," said I, "that would have been worse."

"You would have been forced to go down to the House of Lords," he went on.

"Never!"

"And it might have been fatal. I heard

a debate there, and for weeks I was drowsy, and Tennyson's words ran in my head, —

"'Peers! idle peers! I know not what you mean!'"

"Granting the title is not as bad as it could have been," said I.

"Then you escape the sorrows of a land-lord," said he.

"Is that so?" said I, looking up at him.

"The Irish landlords," said he, as he lit a cigarette, "have no friends but the moon-lighter; for the rest of the world is trying to put them out of their property, while he attempts to put them out of their pain. The Evicted Landlords' Fund—"

"A love of sport," said I, "is one of the chief causes of moonlighting. If people tried to shoot me, I'd have a share of the fun, and go out stalking my enemies."

A Child in the Temple

"If the Irish Question had been invented in the days of the Sphinx, she would be asking it yet," said he.

"Granting it is a lucky escape to have no land," I began.

"You want to travel, and you are not able to do it."

"You call that luck?"

"Countries and actresses look best at a distance. I don't mean to travel till I am dead, then I am going to Mars."

"I don't believe Mars is as bad as all that," said I. "For my part, I want to get away from the winter."

"Well," said he, "a winter in Italy is hardly a success as a summer. I knew a man so determined to be warm that he killed himself. When the coroner's jury heard what a nuisance he had been, they brought in a verdict of 'temporary sanity' to express their approval."

"Look here,—" I began; but he went on with indifference.

"Besides, I suppose you are eager to marry several girls. As you have many disadvantages in your favour, no doubt you could get a wife, but you are luckily poor —"

At this I sighed, and began thinking of Curly.

"You are so young, perhaps you have ambitions," said he. "But they are out of your reach, and you are free from the shame of having earned notoriety by success at the Bar, or by pandering to an irrational public, 'horribilesque ultimosque Britannos,' as Catullus has called them."

"Your words are golden," said I. "Chuck me a cigarette in the interval."

A Child in the Temple

"There are some good writers, of course,"
said he. " 'The Windows in Slums' school
of fiction — "

"Excuse me," said I; "but what on earth
are you driving at?"

"Ah, well," said he, sighing, "youth
meets trouble half-way."

"Trouble?" said I.

"I want you to be content with your lot,"
said he. "What more can you ask? Do you
wish to be a poet? Then verses and re-
verses would be the whole of your history."

"I tell you I am entirely content," I said
pettishly, and regardless of truth.

"In one way you are too much so," said
he, "or you would have opened the window
there, to freshen the room."

"Are you happy now?" I said crossly, as
I opened the window.

Some Guests in the Temple

"A bracing and stiff wind. And now to business," said he briskly, and took a chair at the other side of the table.

"What?" said I dolefully, for I thought I foresaw it. No doubt he would offer a bill of sale on his furniture, for when he borrowed, he loved to pretend it was business, as a check to his conscience.

"Your cousin's will," said he calmly, taking a piece of note-paper out of his breast-pocket, and smoothing it on the table between us.

"So he made one?" said I, with a poor attempt at indifference.

"It is dated last month, and leaves all he possessed to Caterina Moroni."

"I wish her joy of it," said I, with a shrug.

"It is witnessed by two servants who did

not know its effect; and so its secret is ours," he said.

"Much good may it do us!"

"Plenty," said he, "if you are a man of the world."

"How?"

"It was all very well to urge you to be contented," said he; "but it is plain you are not."

"Who is?" said I, crossly. "Are you?"

"Not in the least; and so I propose a bargain," said he.

"What do you mean?"

"If a madman makes a will, it is worthless."

"What then?"

"Your cousin was mad about Caterina Moroni. Besides, he was always crazy, you know."

Some Guests in the Temple

"Terence was your friend," I said, reddening.

"Terence was an unmusical genius," he said. "Men of genius are bells, some musical, and the rest of them cracked. This will is absurd, and the Court would set it aside."

"The Court will not have a chance," said I.

"No," said he; "for I'll do it myself."

"Do," said I, for I thought he was joking.

"That is a good fire," he said calmly. "This paper would be an ash in a moment. But the question is, how much would you give me?"

"You are not in earnest?" said I.

"You will be rich," he went on.

As I sprang up from my chair, the paper was blown down on the carpet.

"This is some joke of yours," I said angrily.

A Child in the Temple

"I was never more in earnest," said he peacefully, taking a cigarette from his case. "The thing would be safe, and a secret from the Law and the Press. The Law and the Press are the ears of England, and grow bigger every day," he went on.

Lord! how I wished he would stop his intolerable attempts to be smart!

"Your ancestors must have been a bad lot," said I.

"They were," said he, as he lit the cigarette and got up. "Then it's no go?"

"I am not old enough yet," said I, with an endeavour to sneer.

"How you will curse yourself, when you come to the age of reason!" said he. "But where is the will?" he went on in a sharper voice.

"On the floor," said I crossly.

"It's not there," said he, stooping, and then he made a rush for the dog.

Seeing him come, she fled away with delight, and enjoyed the game so, it took him a time to get the paper again. Then she hung on to his trousers, with pretended ferocity. It was lucky for her I was not out of the room. Foster was purple, and his calmness was gone.

"This is your boasted honour, no doubt?" said he.

"What have I done now?" I said pleasantly.

"That beast has eaten the signatures!" he cried, as if he wanted to kill her.

"Poor thing!" said I; "she must have been hungry."

"It is your doing!" he cried.

"Nonsense! You know I didn't taste the wretched will," I said angrily.

A Child in the Temple

"It is my belief you have trained the brute to eat signatures," he cried, in a frenzy.

"I wish I could," I replied. "She would be worth her weight in gold in the City."

There was a timorous knocking, and he opened the door, as if he looked for a victim. I heard Mrs. Maclean telling him a lady had asked for him; and then he went out, and his voice was sweet on the landing. Then I could hear him usher somebody in, — and there was Kitty Moroney.

"My friend, Lord Kilmorna," said Foster, in his affable way.

"We have met before," she said, holding out her hand with a smile.

"Yes, indeed," said I, taking her hand with a good deal of embarrassment.

Some Guests in the Temple

"You have changed very little," said she, "though you look quieter now."

"Was he ever recklessly wild?" said Foster.

"But you find me changed, I am sure," she said to me with a questioning look, as if at heart she was grave.

"Well, I have seen you lately," said I.

"At the theatre?" she said, flushing a little.

"Yes, several times."

"Do you know, I fancied I saw you?" she said, "but you had altered so little, I was sure it couldn't be you."

"My brain reels," said Foster. "Spare me these Celtic subtleties: you know I am English."

"You make me tired," she said pettishly, and looked at the room. "So this is where

A Child in the Temple

you live?" she went on, to me. "What a
dark quiet old room it is!—and just like a
bookshop. And just fancy! there's not a
sign of a looking-glass."

"I can get you one," said I, with a blush.

"Oh, how dreadfully literal you are!" she
said laughingly. "You were always like
that. I only wondered, because I know men
spend most their time at their mirrors.
And is this your dear little dog?" she went
on, stooping, and fondling Mab, who was trying to tear a hole in her cloak.

Though I know little of dress, I could see
the cloak was a marvel of fur, and in the
height of fashion. Her red cheeks and
bright eyes were at their best amid the
bookish surroundings. No matter where
she might go, Kitty could never seem out
of place. Just as roses become a garret,

she was fair in this room; and I felt I could never again think it was only fit for a companion of folios. The fire put all the room in a glow, and did as well as a lamp.

There came another knock at the door, and Foster answered it, with his usual loftiness.

"It seems so strange to meet you like this," Kitty was saying; and then she drew back with a little cry of astonishment.

Looking to see what had startled her, I turned to the door. Two nuns were coming into the room, and Foster was there, grinning behind them. The first was a little withered old nun, with a pinched and pitying face. A taller one followed her; and I could not believe my eyes, — for it was Curly Adair.

"Mr. Fenton?" the little nun said doggedly, in a quavering voice, as if she was accustomed to begging, and detested it still.

At the best of times, I am easily put out of countenance, and now I was crimson. Curly had started, as if she had been delighted to see me; and then, as she recognised Kitty, her look suddenly froze. Finding her here now, she was unjust to us both. Glancing at Kitty, I saw her staring at Curly with a tragical white face, as if she looked at a ghost.

"You are Mr. Fenton, I think," said the old nun, and her voice came as if she stood at a distance.

"No, I am not," I stammered, glad to have something to say while I collected my thoughts.

"But that is the name on the door."

"Mine is on a card underneath it. I have his rooms while he is out in America."

"But your man told us we would find him in here — "

I looked at Foster, and as he heard what she said, he reeled as if he was struck.

"He is a stupid fellow," I said; "I think I'll have to discharge him."

"Then," she said timidly, "I have made a mistake."

"I am afraid so," said I, and I hoped Curly suspected she was making one also.

"But if there is anything I can do — " I went on.

"Well," said the nun, "Mr. Fenton was on my list as a man who gave us help for our poor."

A Child in the Temple

"You must let me do what I can," said I, getting a sovereign out of my pocket.

"What name shall I put down on the list?" said she, as she took the money with thanks.

But at this I faced Curly, who stood cold and sedate, with her hands clasped, and her eyes set on the ground.

"You have not forgotten me altogether, I hope," said I, and my voice quavered as the nun's had been doing.

"I beg your pardon," she said gently, and faced me as if she thought me a stranger.

"My name is Burke," I said, conscious I was growing redder, if possible; "that is, it is Kilmorna, I mean."

Curly nodded her stately head graciously, as much as to say, "Indeed! how delightful!

If your name had been Moses, it would have interested me as much and as little."

"You must forgive us for our intrusion," she said sweetly. "I need not tell you I regret the mistake."

With that she turned to the door.

"What name shall I write?" the little nun quavered, and peered as if she thought I was crazy, as I had been mentioning two.

"Any name! any name!" I cried in agony, and turned to the window.

"You young people appeared taken aback," Foster said, when he had shut the door after them.

"You don't understand," said Kitty, as if she was making an effort. "We knew one of the Sisters."

"You knew her also?" said Foster. "She

seemed to think she had known enough of Kilmorna."

Kitty went on: "And my sister is a nun in that convent. 'Sister Mercy' is her name in religion. So they reminded me of a number of things."

"What a pity she did n't come, instead of the old lady!" said Foster. "What a dramatic opportunity wasted!"

"I must go now," she said, as if he jarred on her then. "Come," she went on, to me, as I stared at the snow, "you have no call to be downcast. I know I ought to have said or done something—and yet, what could I do?"

"Nothing is so dramatic as silence," said Foster.

"So you showed, when they thought you were my footman," said I, with an attempt to be light.

Some Guests in the Temple

"She did n't look at me; and she must be short-sighted," he answered crossly, as Kitty said good-bye and went out.

But as soon as he had followed her out, she came again to the threshold.

"Look here," she said, "I 'll make it all right."

"Oh, it does n't matter at all," said I, airily; "don't bother about it."

"Oh, you poor child!" she said laughingly, and with that she was gone.

I went and sat in my deck-chair, without stirring for some time; and as I looked at the flames, I thought of nothing at all, but was miserable, and my throat and my eyes were sore, and I could have cried heartily if I had not been a man. When I am cheerful, I am assured of my manhood, and long for an occasion for my preposterous courage; but in my moments of gloom, I am a baby again. Or am I always a child, and only able to act manliness when my heart is at ease?

Meanwhile, Mab, on my knees, sighed bitterly, as if she was sure there were no cutlets for dinner.

"This will never do, Mab," said I, as I put her down on the floor respectfully; for her spirit is high, and I have never been rude to her.

"You and I are grown up," said I solemnly. "You are a year old, I believe, and I twenty-one; and so we ought to be hardened. I am going to work, and that is the reason I have to put you away from me."

"All right," she said with her tail, and lay at ease on the rug.

Some Guests in the Temple

So I lit my lamp, and disguised it with the pleated green shade that Foster says makes it look as if it was dancing a ballet; but still I left the window ajar, because I felt fevered, and the air was refreshing; and besides, there was a lingering scent of something Kitty had used, and I was ungallant enough to want to be rid of that disturbing reminder.

Sitting down at my long desk, I took up the manuscript of my Treatise on Bills. That was a subject I had chosen, as I knew nothing about it; and so I was not confused by remembering contradictory cases.

But now I could not abide it, and so I took out the little volume of verses I had made on the sly. It opened at the verses that came to me when I should have been listening to the Dean in the Abbey: —

A Child in the Temple

"You, in this crowded solitude, recall
  Despairing hopes forgotten men bequeath:
I wonder what they think about it all, —
  That silent congregation underneath."

"Idiotic!" I muttered, and turned over
the page: —

" The cuckoo wanders in the woods again,
  And calls deplorably: I think he grieves
For some unfaithful friend he seeks in vain, —
  Or has he lost himself among the leaves?"

So far I read; and then I groaned with
remorse, and threw the lot in the fire.
Then I decided to write a letter to some
one. But I felt I disliked every one; and so
I sat idle, and stared out of the window, till
a thought came to me, and I said to myself I
would write to Curly, explaining everything;
but then I was angered. "I 'll explain nothing at all," said I. "And if she wrongs me

so much — it can't be helped, I suppose, and it does n't matter to me." But I knew well there was nothing mattered so much. Then said I to myself, "It would be an odd love-letter, and the first I have written: I suppose I 'll never write one at all."

There was the sheet of paper in front of me, and I had nothing to do. So the whim took me to write a love-letter now in spite of Destiny, and make believe Curly could be mine, after all, and tear it up when the illusion was over. I found it easy to write, for there was much in my heart. Saying nothing about the convent, or my penniless lot, — for I was making believe the dividing work of our fates was undone, — I told her how much I cared for her, and asked her to marry me, even though I was small, and had not grown a moustache as big as Sergeant Molloy's. 77

A Child in the Temple

Then I put my love-letter into an envelope, and wrote the address in a large handwriting with ridiculous flourishes, —

"THE REVEREND SISTER CURLY ADAIR,
JERUSALEM HOUSE,
HAMMERSMITH,
EUROPE."

and then I scribbled above, —

"HASTE ! HASTE ! POST HASTE !"

as people did in old times.

So I looked at that address, and grinned ruefully, and felt I was having a sad little joke at my own expense ; and as I was saying, "So much for my first and last love-letter," somebody came and knocked at the door. I wanted to read the letter through, and im-agine how Curly would have received it ; so putting it face downwards, I went to see who was there.

CHAPTER III

ADESTE FIDELES

FOSTER strode in with the tragical dignity he has learnt in the theatres.

"She has wonderful eyes," he said, sighing, as he looked down upon Mab.

"And her legs are so refined," I said dreamily, as I went to my chair, and watched Mab, who was feigning to be asleep in the fender, for fear I should summon her out of it if I knew she was waking.

"She is gracefulness itself," he went on, as if he had not heard my remark.

"And yet she feels so plump when you pinch her," said I.

A Child in the Temple

"Then she is a bright little girl: at times she has gleams of almost human intelligence," he sighed, as if he talked to himself, while he paused, in an absent-minded way, to fill up his cigarette-case again with the Melachrinos I foolishly left out on the table.

"At all times," I corrected.

"No," he said firmly. "There are times when she is merely emotional; but when the moon is not up, she has an undesirable insight into the manners of men."

"Ah! she is too trusting," I sighed, and remembered how I dreaded the thieves.

"There is more sense than you think in that little head of hers, though she looks so airy and light," he said.

"Does n't she look light?" I replied. "But she feels heavy enough."

"What do you mean?" he said, starting.

"When I took her boating at Halliford, I thought she had been dining on lead," said I.

"You took her boating?" he said incredulously.

"I don't mean in the dead of winter," said I pettishly. "It was last summer; and she wouldn't be still, but kept running up and down in the boat."

"Kept running up and down? You are raving," he said.

"She did indeed," said I, "and sometimes when she is here on my knees for a couple of hours, my legs are numb from her weight."

"Who on earth are you talking about?" he said savagely.

"Why, Mab, of course," I replied.

"I am talking about Kitty Moroney!" he shrieked.

A Child in the Temple

" Kitty Moroney ! " I cried aghast, as I thought of the remarks I had made.

" You have that mongrel cur on the brain," he went on, with ferocity. " I have a mind to throw her out of the window."

"Don't" said I bitterly. " You 'll find it a long fall to the ground."

Here another knock came, and he strode across to the door.

" Well, what do you want? " he shouted as he opened it fiercely.

" I vant ze zings," said Allessandro, dismayed.

" Take the things, reptile ! " cried Foster ; and Allessandro slunk in.

This Allessandro is a waiter, — a dark pathetic and thieving Italian, whose elaborate ignorance of English defends him when he is caught in a robbery. No one can make as subtle mistakes. The other night, when my dinner was an hour or so late, he smiled with such sadness as he said, " I 'av forgive," when he ought to have said he had forgotten, that I joined in forgiveness. Now he had come to fetch the plates I had used at lunch, and as he took them up, Foster went on angrily, —

" I came here on business."

" Again?" said I, with a groan.

" Not that nonsense of the will," said he savagely. " It is serious, I tell you."

" That was serious enough," said I dolefully.

" Will you let me speak?" he cried sternly.

"Yes, but do try to speak a little softer," I said.

Foster rushed out, and slammed the door as he went.

" Sair," said Allessandro, as he was piling

the things on a tray, " I 'ave a friend vot is seeck."

" So have I," said I to myself.

" My friend vant you to come to 'eem," said Allessandro, with pathos.

" Indeed? " said I crossly. " I am sorry I can't"

" My friend dyin'," said Allessandro, with gloom.

" Lucky chap ! " said I to myself.

" Eem Irlandese," the small waiter went on.

" Irish? " said I, starting, " that 's a different thing. Why did n't you say so before? "

" 'E come from your town."

" From Ballymorna? " said I.

" Dot 's eet," he said earnestly.

" What 's his name? " said I.

" Not know," he replied.

Adeste Fideles

"You don't know your friend's name?" I said suspiciously.

"Eet longissimo," he said with a shrug.

I let that pass, as some names in my part of the country might seem a little uncouth.

"What's wrong with him?" said I.

"Tisica."

"Consumption?" said I. "Poor fellow! He wants to see me, you say?"

"Vary soon," said the waiter.

"And where does he live?" said I.

"Tree, Vindsor Street, Soho," he said promptly, as if he was repeating a lesson.

"All right, I'll go and see him," I said, as I got up from the chair.

"Vary soon?" said the waiter.

"Now," said I, for I was glad of the chance of finding something to do.

So I went into my bedroom, and put on

my coat and hat, and took my umbrella,
and dropped my revolver into my right-hand
pocket as usual. Allessandro let himself out,
and that took him some time, as he had to
balance his tray, so I was little behind him.

As I was crossing the threshold, the wind
slammed the door, and with a horrible oath
— instinctive, but not put into words — I was
thrust out on the landing. This did not
better my mood, nor did a meeting with
Foster, who was there, and received me
with a satirical gravity.

" You come out quickly," said he.

" I am in a hurry," said I sulkily, shutting
the outer door of my chambers.

" Then I hope you are going the same way
as the wind," said he.

Without answering this silly remark, I was
going by, but he said, —

Adeste Fideles

"I want to see you on business."

"I have no time now," I said crossly.

"It's important," said he.

"Can't it wait?" I said peevishly.

"Not long," said he.

"Well, where can I meet you?" said I, hastily deciding to spend all my loose cash before I saw him again.

"At Covent Garden, at six," said he.

"Theatre?"

"Nonsense!" said he, fretfully, "at that time of the day! The market, of course."

"Where they sell potatoes?" I said more cheerfully, as I seemed to annoy him.

"And simpletons. At this end of the gallery," he said.

"Oh, yes," I said innocently, "the place where you're on show every day. All right; I'll be there at six."

A Child in the Temple

As I went on, I heard Mab's clattering
chain upon the staircase below. I caught up
Allessandro outside, and he told me she was
safe with Maclean. A hansom was there,
and I took it, and he gave the address; and
I noticed the driver was an acquaintance of
his.

By this time it was dark: and it was beginning to snow. The lamps and windows
were lit in the Strand, and they were shining
on snowy umbrellas and the watery pavement. The steady crowds in the Strand were
hurrying in fear of a storm.

In the black unsavoury roads northwards
there was nothing to watch; and so, no
longer intent on that unflagging romance
of a crowd, I could consider my errand, and
wonder who the man was, and run over the
names of the people that used to live in

the village. I was so employed, when the
cab drew up with a jerk; and as I leapt
to the ground, and paid the fare, I could
see nobody stirring.

The house was dingy, and so when I had
rung, I said to myself there were lodgings,
and I would find the sick man in a respectable garret. The door opened, and a man
was inside; but he was dim, for it was dark
in the hall.

"Well, what do you want?" he said
gruffly.

"My name is Kilmorna."

"You are expected," said he, and, standing aside, made way for me, then, closing
the door, knocked at another at the end of
the passage.

The door opened, with a clatter of voices,
and then he whispered to some one; and

there was silence as he turned to me, saying, "This way," and I went into the room.

The room was naked and long, and lit by gas flaring in flaunting jets on the walls. Men sat crowding a long table, and turned to me; and so I fancied I was shown in by mistake.

" I was told — " I began.

"We know that," said an old man on my right, at the head of the table, with his back to the door. "The question is, what you will tell us."

He was a tall fellow in black, with a tangle of white hair, and a heavy moustache, and I thought him a Swede; for he had frosty blue eyes and a strong colour, and though his English was good, his accent came from abroad.

" I came to see a sick man," said I.

"You can see several here," said he. "Now, there is little health in the world."

As he spoke, he was leaning his right elbow on the table, and propping his head, while he studied me with glittering eyes.

"Let me pass," said I, impatiently, turning to the man who had shown me in; but he leant against the door and replied, "Later on," in a dull menacing way. He had a hairy dark face, and a cropped beard, and I thought him undesirably strong. No doubt he was a foreigner also, but he might have been anything that was unpleasant and dangerous.

"Do you know who we are?" said the old man.

"I don't know, and I don't care," I said flippantly.

Said he scowling: "When I tell you the

name of this Society, you will care a good deal."

" I don't want to know it," said I.

" Will you be silent? " said he sternly. " You will answer our questions, and take an oath of secrecy about all you may hear and any members you see."

" No, I won't," said I.

"My little young man," said he calmly, " I beg you will not make a mistake. This is a matter of life and death with you now."

"Indeed!" said I airily; though I began to be cold, as if I stood in a draught.

Said he: "We have learnt the little value of life; and so we risk it and take it with unaffected indifference."

There was something prosy and practical in his manner that was very depressing.

"Nihilists," said I to myself, " or Anarch-

ists, or one of the similar playful little socie-
ties," as I looked at the others. They were
shabby and weary, and by no means romantic; and their stolid attention disconcerted
me hugely.

"Forgive me," said I politely. "But I
think the mistake is yours; for I have nothing to do with you."

"Now," he went on, as if I had not spoken
at all, "these are the questions you are to
answer in full."

"And if I refuse?" said I.

"You will not refuse very long," said he,
with such meaning that I made up my mind
I would get out if I could. I did not choose
to be menaced into answering any questions
they liked, and my revolver was handy. I
saw no weapons about, though I took it for
granted they had a number in reach.

A Child in the Temple

"Where is Lord Kilmorna?" said he.

I was so taken aback by this question that I opened my mouth and stared; and he repeated it slowly.

"You mean my cousin?" said I.

"Do you refuse to answer?" he said.

"You are behind the times," I said affably.

"My little young man," said he very quietly, "I have warned you enough. This is the last chance I shall give you. Where is Lord Kilmorna?"

"Don't you know my cousin is dead?" said I hurriedly.

The man at the door stepped forward, but I sprang at him, crying, "Back!" and snatching out my revolver, fired it full in his face; and as he staggered away from me, I was out of the room in a second, and across the small passage, and undoing the bolt. Cries were behind me, and as I got the door open, men rushed into the passage. "Stop him! Don't fire at him!" they were shouting, as I was reaching the road. Then my legs ran away with me, till I found myself breathless in an alley remote from those inquisitive people.

"So much for benevolence," I gasped, as I dropped the revolver into my pocket, and put my hat straight, and looked ruefully at the mud on my boots. "Never again will I go and visit the sick."

That dim alley was still, for it was between the backs of big gloomy buildings; and so I was able to take my time, and recover breath, while I looked for another way to get out. Such a way was up in the left corner, and under a black arch; and so, trying it, I got suddenly into the light

A Child in the Temple

of St. Martin's Lane, among a medley of passers.

Looking at my watch, I discovered it was near six, and so I beckoned a hansom, and told the driver to take me to Covent Garden; and on the road I was trying to guess what that singular scene and question had meant, but I had made nothing out of it when I got to the market. There I found a great many people, and much business astir in the open, where the boxes of oranges and lemons and dried fruit, and the masses of vegetables, lay, while inside the long gallery of the flower-shops, the windows were all red with the roses newly come from the South. As I looked vainly for Foster, I went along to the west end of the gallery; and there I came on a couple of tattered Italians, standing out in the slush, with a barrel organ the man worked, while the woman was chanting the hymn "Adeste Fideles."

The woman was still young, and her dress was such as one sees when the dust is like smoke on the shining roads of the South, and the olives along the wayside are white, and the lizards bask in the sun, and the grasshoppers clash their shrill monotonous cymbals. Here, in this winter darkness of London, she startled me, and so did her song, for it carried my thoughts to our little church in the village, where once the rector's wife taught me to join in the English form of those verses, "Come, let us adore Him," at Christmas, when I was small. I remembered the chilly church, and the twilight of the only lamp that was lit, for money was scarce, and the dripping wreaths of the ivy we gathered out in the rain, and the rector's wife,

A Child in the Temple

an unwieldy grandmotherly woman, who could not sing in the least, though that mattered the less since it was not seldom the hearts of the poor sang at her coming. All of a sudden, I had a glimpse of the windy moors and black stooping woods and grey lawns, where the folds of the mist shook like a curtain or hurried like ghosts, and I was dry for that welcome and immaculate air.

After the lonely and fresh fields of my country I saw the market again, and those disconsolate exiles; and I turned to my neighbours, and wondered whether that tune could clutch their throats as it did mine, and enable them to see the old places through a mist in their eyes.

But most the bystanders were stolid people, and I was turning away, when I saw

Adeste Fideles

Kitty Moroney.   Dressed in her furs and at-
tended by her man with a burden of roses,
she stood there on my left, by the step of her
neat carriage, and watched the woman singing before us.   For her, at least, it was plain
the timely song had a spell; and my heart
went out to her then in sympathy, for her
eyes had a sadness and her face a despairing
whiteness I was sorry to see.   Yet there
was something more familiar about her than
there was when she was rosy and blithe; and
I thought she had that loftier look I had seen
when she was only a child.

The hymn was done, and the organ, without stopping, jerked off into the jingling
absurdity popular in the music-halls then.
So the knot of bystanders grew; but Kitty,
giving her servant a coin for the singer, and
telling her coachman he need not wait any

more, but could go back to the house, went
on alone in the dark.

Her voice seemed altered and strained, as
if she was in trouble, and this made me the
more eager to talk to her, since perhaps I
could help, — and anyway I wanted to tell her
all the money was hers. For all I knew,
money matters might plague her, and so
here was my chance to put her at rest, instead of letting her spoil her Christmas
season with care. So I followed her, thinking she would go into some shop the other
side of the market, and I could watch her
come out, and pretend to meet her by accident; but she went down Maiden Lane, and
turned into a door on the left, and I saw the
place was a chapel.

I heard singing inside, and going down
some black steps, and then pushing a heavy

door on the right of the little hall, I looked into a chapel where many children were kneeling, as if a girls' school had been brought there to a service. There among them knelt Kitty; and so I took a chair at the back, where I was out of her sight. The old building was dark; but wreaths and loops were aloft, and the big pillars were prominent in glimmering ivy. A priest in vestments with much gold on them was ending a service: and the air had that alien and drowsy savour of incense. Many and misty candles were shining above the altar, though near me the light was faint, for the gas was burning badly; but Kitty was clear, for she was under a lamp. As she knelt there among some very small girls, and looked at that gleaming altar, the children stood up and began singing the hymn "Adeste

A Child in the Temple

Fideles," and she stooped forward and hid her face in her hands.

The priest, an old man with a sorrowful and womanish voice, knelt and said prayers, pausing till the children repeated them. I remembered one of the prayers, since I had heard it at home, when Curly used to beguile me into the chapel; for all the people were friends in our village, and the priest and the rector sat down together, being kind fellows both, and united by a singular zeal for the propagation of horses.

"Hail, holy Queen, Mother of Mercy!" it began, and that shrill chorus repeated the words; and the old priest quavered, "Our life, our Sweetness, and our Hope," and then he paused for the children; and when they had done, went on, "To thee do we cry, poor banished children of Eve," and waited again for that young echo, and proceeded, "To thee do we send up our sighs, weeping and wailing in this valley of tears," and then, "Turn, then, most gracious Advocate, thine eyes of mercy towards us, and after this our exile" — but that was all I heard then, for I saw Kitty was crying.

Then the service was over, and the children came trooping down the dim aisle; they had all the same dress of dark blue, and I think they must have come from an orphanage. Two nuns were in charge, and soon the clatter of small feet had died out; and Kitty and I were left alone in the place. But it was not for long, as she got up and went out; and I hurried to speak to her, but was only in time to see her enter a hansom.

The driver was elderly, with a wrinkled

and shaven face, and had the air of a jockey;
and as she stood up in the front part of the
hansom, he leant forward towards her with
a grin, as if he knew who she was without
respecting her much. I daresay he did not
know her at all, but was misled by her looks
and her weakness for elaborate clothes. Be
that as it may, I saw her wince from his
look as if she felt it an insult, and she spoke
faltering, and then he grinned wider, with a
friendly impertinence.

"Jerusalem 'Ouse? Why, Miss, that's a
convent," said he, as if she made a mistake.

She stood still for a moment, looking up
at his leering face, as if the man was a type
of all the people she knew; and then she
said suddenly, —

"No, not the convent. Drive to the
Temple — I mean the pier on the River."

Adeste Fideles

The snow had stopped, and the pavement was slippery as I made my way home along the Strand to the Temple. I soon gave up wondering what on earth she could want at the pier at such an hour, for I found it was useless; and so I thought about Foster, and decided to lend him a sovereign in the hope he might give me a dinner out of it, and so I should celebrate Christmas without feeling extravagant.

As I got to the house, Mab skurried to meet me, and jumped up on me wildly.

"She knows she's been a good dog," said Maclean, as I stooped to answer her welcome.

"She always is," said I.

"Ah, it's the letter she is so proud about now!" said he.

"What letter?" said I.

A Child in the Temple

"The one you gave her to post, my lord."

"When?" said I, wondering.

"Just before you went out, she ran down here with a letter, as you taught her to do."

"To-day?" said I, and a fear was like a knife in my heart.

"And we sent it off by a boy, because the mails are so slow at Christmas, and we saw you had written 'haste,' on the top."

Never in my life have I known the agony and despair of that moment. I saw it all at a glance; my letter to Curly had been blown down on the carpet of my room by the wind, and the dog had carried it off, when the waiter opened the door.

"It was a letter to Jerusalem House, my lord. It will have got there by now."

"Good dog! good dog!" said I, in a choking voice, and I turned and I went out of the

house.   I could not face the Macleans, or
the dog, or a light, but had to keep in the
dark.

As I passed under the archway, and so
through the gardens to the Embankment, I
knew what people felt when they jumped
into the Thames.   I had written a love-letter
to Curly: it would be opened by the Reverend Mother.   I had addressed it to ' The
Reverend Sister Curly ': they would think
I was mad.   All I can say is, I hope few
in the world have ever suffered as I did.
Heaven only knows how long I was pacing
about the dusky Embankment.   Then I felt
I must talk about anything else to take my
mind from that horror.   I could not face
those who knew about the letter, and least
of all that well-meaning criminal Mab, but
I could speak to a stranger.

A Child in the Temple

"What boat is that?" said I, tragically, to a man who was leaning on the wall by the River.

"That launch? It is the 'Iniquity,' sir," said he, and I saw he was one of the fellows who are in charge of the pier.

"Who has her now?" said I; for that was Terence's launch.

"Mr. Foster, a young gent in the Temple," said he, "and he has just gone on board."

So I went down to the pier and across the gangway on to the launch, to look for Foster, and find why it was there, and what he wanted me for; but I saw no one on deck, and then I thought a light on the bank started, and I knew we were off.

CHAPTER IV

ON BOARD THE " INIQUITY "

BLACKFRIAR'S BRIDGE appeared to be wading along the trough of the Thames. I stood irresolute, and the River was dark, till we shot under the bridge, and beyond its shadow the lights of vessels were plentiful and mirrored by misty stars upon the shimmering water.

On my right was the cabin, and I heard voices below. As we were passing the bridge, I heard a ringing and young laugh, and I was sure it was Kitty's. I daresay it was only my fancy; but I thought there was something

A Child in the Temple

more reckless in it now than there was when
its light-heartedness set her many worshippers
smiling. What had brought her on board,
and where could she be going with Foster?
Remembering how she had told the cabman
to drive to the Temple, as if she was making
a choice between extremes, I reflected Jerusalem House and the launch "Iniquity" had
little in common. I had never a doubt of her
goodness; but I feared she adventured rashly
with that man of the world. I counted Kitty
a friend, though I was nothing to her. So I
stepped forward to go down to the cabin,
since my being there would be enough to
interfere with his plans, if he was aiming at
mischief. But I ran into him, just as I was
reaching the stairs.

"Who the devil — ?" he said, peering down
at me because it was dark.

On Board the "Iniquity"

"Hullo, Foster, is that you?" said I affably.

"Baby Bunting!" he cried out, in astonishment.

At this I crimsoned with rage, for I already suspected he had christened me "Bunting." My indignation was such, I was not able to speak.

"How did you get here?" he went on.

"Is Miss Moroney on board?" I said, choking, with an attempt to be calm.

"What's that to you?" he said angrily.

"Answer my question!" I cried, in a most truculent tone.

"*You* won't be on board very long,' said he, "for I'll put you off, at that pier: and then you can run home and have a game with your dog."

Maddened at this insult, I sprang on him,

and thrust my revolver up to his forehead, and cried, " Silence, ruffian ! " and in that moment the deadliest of my dreams was fulfilled. It is true I had never dreamt Foster would be the man I should menace; but he did very well.

"Well, I am —— ! " he exclaimed in unaffected astonishment, and leapt back, and fell over something, and I sprang down the steps to the cabin, and I very near went head foremost, for the staircase was steep.

So I crashed against the door of the cabin with unintentional violence; and I strode in, for I was not able to stop. Though I was hatless, and it was hard to transform my floundering to a dignified entry, I felt as if I was charging into a cabin where mad and desperate pirates were feasting, as I had always resolved to do when my adventures began.

I was dazzled at first, for the narrow cabin was painted with white and gold, and ablaze with electric lamps that were doubled by many mirrors about. Then I saw people at the table before me. One of them was Kitty, of course; but as I looked at the other, a big soldierly fellow, with a black twisted preposterous moustache, and a reckless and young face, and dark wavy hair fringed by grey shadows, it is no wonder I gasped, for it was Terence himself.

They seemed thunderstruck also, till Terence shouted a laugh, and leapt up from his seat with a cry of, —

"Larry, my son! A merry Christmas, my boy! You are as welcome as a rose in December."

A Child in the Temple

"Terence!" I cried, "is it you? Oh, Terence! Terence! I believed you were dead."

I would have hugged him, if there had been nobody looking. But he cared nothing for any watcher, and flung his arms about me as he said with a laugh, —

"Why, Larry, my son, I do believe you are glad I have not gone out after all! Come along," he cried, pulling me off to the other end of the table; "whatever hour a man comes, he is in time for a drink. You know Lady Kilmorna, don't you?"

"Lady Kilmorna?" I said in renewed astonishment, and hid my revolver in my pocket, as I turned towards Kitty.

"Of course!" and he shouted laughing again, "You had n't heard of our marriage? Dear, dear, I meant to invite you to come and act as a bridesmaid!"

On Board the "Iniquity"

But Kitty was quiet, and reddened as she avoided my eyes.

"I am awfully glad," said I — and I was, too, for it seemed the best way out of it all.

My tone seemed to amuse Terence, for he went on with his deafening laughter, as he made me sit down.

"Well, you are a quaint little shrimp," he said. "You should be framed as a picture of a benevolent infancy."

"But I thought you were dead," I said again, as the wine frothed in my glass.

"So I was," said he pleasantly.

"And when did you come to life?" said I cheerfully.

"I am dead still," he answered me, in a tragical tone.

"And how did you come to die?" said I carelessly.

A Child in the Temple

"It is a secret, my son," said he solemnly; and at this I was hurt he would not trust it to me, so I looked towards Kitty, and saw her flushed and embarrassed, with her eyes on the flowers on the table, as if her thoughts were aloof.

"I was humbugging, Larry," said Terence, with his hand on my shoulder. "My dear, I'll tell you, of course."

But Kitty got up, and said the cabin was close, and she would go upon deck. As we got up from our chairs, Terence proposed we should go with her; but she made him stop down, saying she would walk for a little with Foster and come back to us then.

"The fact is," said Terence, as he shut the door after her and came back to his seat, "I am in trouble, as usual."

"Indeed," said I, with sympathy.

"Well, that is the wrong way to put it," said he cheerfully. "When people say I am in trouble, it only means the police are in it, most of the time."

"The police?" said I, with alarm.

"At every station and pier," said he, "stolid detectives are looking out for me vainly: I am glad to give a pleasant employment to those respectable men. When a policeman has won a reputation for quietness and teaching a Sunday-school, he is made a detective."

"You are a criminal then?" said I calmly, to show I was a man of the world.

"A plotter."

"At 3 Windsor Street, Soho?"

"The very place. You never saw such a set."

"Oh, yes, I, did," said I sadly; and I told

him about my scene with that gang, and it amused him immensely.

"But what induced you to join them?" said I.

"Life was so dull," said he; "and I wanted those fellows to blow up the Irish members of all politics, as a plea for Home Rule."

"But you abandoned that dream?" said I.

"They abandoned me to the police," he said sadly; "they began to think I was humorous."

"And so?" said I.

"I feigned death," he said tragically.

"And you have been in hiding?" I said.

"Under the false name of Muldoon, for fear any one should suppose I was Irish."

"And that will?" said I.

On Board the "Iniquity"

"Foster and I had a little bet," said he affably. "He said you were too good to be true; and so we planned the will as a test. 'Where there's a will, there's a way,' said he; but he had to own he was wrong."

"You might have let me know you were safe," said I.

"Well," said he. "I wrote you a letter: you would have found it to-morrow. By-the-bye, you know you are welcome, — but how on earth did you join us?"

"I got on, at the Temple," said I.

"Why?"

"Foster wanted to speak to me."

"Yes, I told him to let you into our secret; but did he welcome you here?"

"He wanted to put me off," said I sadly.

"And you would n't go?"

A Child in the Temple

" I thought Lady Kilmorna was here alone with him," said I, blushing, and looking hard at the table.

"Larry," said he, after a pause, "you are a remarkable child. I am beginning to think you will be a man after all. But it will take some time yet; and you must study the world."

"I know it quite well enough," said I, flushing again; for if there is one thing I hate, it is to have people think I am innocent.

"True for you, Larry," said he, laughing, but rather sadly, I thought. "Little is enough in the weariness of the knowledge of life. Look here, I wish you would go and live at Kilmorna."

"At Kilmorna?" said I, starting.

"Marry some little girl over there," he

went on; "I daresay you'll find one about as green as yourself, when you have searched a long time."

"This is not the way there."

"No, this is the way to Boulogne."

"You are going across?"

"Not in this launch," said he. "I have the yacht at Sheerness."

"Well, then, I'll come back in the launch."

"As you like; but if you do, I daresay you'll be arrested," said he.

"Oh, I rather like the police," said I carelessly.

"You do, do you?" said Foster savagely, as he entered the cabin. "Well, that's a good thing; for you'll have enough of them soon." It was plain he was still sore at the thought of my unconventional conduct. "The police are making us stop," he went on; and we sprang up from our seats.

"Oh, what will we do?" cried Kitty, standing beside him.

"Make a fight for it," Terence said joyously, "and get away down the River. You must stop down here, little girl."

Said Foster, "I have a plan."

"Oh, how clever you are!" cried Kitty, full of relief.

"You stop down below — " he went on, to Terence.

"I think I see myself, sir!" said Terence, with sublime indignation.

"Their warrant will be for Lord Kilmorna, of course; so we'll give up this little animal here," Foster went on grimly, and caught me by the back of the neck.

"Leave go!" I cried crossly, resenting

his familiar behaviour. "You'll give me up
to the police?" I went on, scowling, as I got
from his grasp.

"And it will teach you not to fool with
revolvers and grown-up people again," he
said bitterly.

"Rubbish!" said Terence. "And do you
think I'd agree?"

But as he spoke, I changed my mind in
a second. "You must," said I; "when they
get me on shore they will find out their
mistake."

"You must, indeed, dear," said Kitty.

Said Foster, "This child here will be use-
ful for once; and then a policeman can take
him home in a cab. Think what a good
joke it will be."

"And you know I want to go back,"
said I.

A Child in the Temple

Said Foster, " That's a good thing."

" Faith, it will be a joke," said Terence, with his echoing laugh. " And they can't hurt you at all, Larry, — and you want to go home. New Scotland Yard is near enough to the Temple. Here are my thickest furs," he went on, taking a heavy coat from a lounge. " Stand on tip-toe, and talk to them in a dangerous voice."

" Quick, now," said Foster, as I put on the big coat and a cap that came down over my eyes, and he caught my left wrist, and hauled me off, while the others were laughing at something, — perhaps at his unmannerly violence.

" Stand on that coil of rope," he went on, as he pulled me up on the deck, " and try to look like a man."

I would not condescend to answer him,

but got up on a coil of rope beside the head
of the staircase.

"It makes you a proper height, I declare,"
he said.

"And it gave you your proper position,"
said I. "For I had the satisfaction of seeing
you tumble over it lately."

"Shut up!" said he savagely. "Though
you are three quarters a girl, you wouldn't
be a bad little simpleton, if you would only
be quiet. But the way you prattle —"

"Prattle!" I cried fiercely, clutching my
revolver again.

Then Kitty came up the stairs, and I heard
voices beside the launch, on the right, and a
tug slid alongside, and ropes were thrown,
and a gangway was thrust out, and a sergeant
and some other policemen came on board the
"Iniquity." Four or five of them came, and

A Child in the Temple

one was holding a bull's eye lantern; and as I saw it, I muffled my face again in the fur.

"What does all this mean?" said Foster.

"Lord Kilmorna?" said the sergeant politely.

"That is not my name," he replied.

"I thought not," the sergeant said calmly; and then in a business-like indifferent way, — "I have a warrant for Lord Kilmorna," said he.

"Nonsense, my good fellow," said Foster loftily; but the policeman broke in very quietly, —

"Don't let us waste any time. Lord Kilmorna must come with us; and there is an end of it."

"Where is your warrant?" I said in a voice so thrilling and deep that even Foster was startled: and every one looked at me, and the man with the lantern turned its light on my face.

" That hain't the man," said he solemnly.

" Do you know Lord Kilmorna by sight?" said Foster.

" No," said the sergeant, " but I have read his description."

" The description must have been right, so of course you 'll let us go on," said Foster.

" After a little search," the policeman said mildly. " I won't delay you a minute."

" Search away then," said Foster, and at something the sergeant said, the constables scattered in other parts of the launch.

" Come along, Kilmorna," said Foster, " and let us finish the game."

" Your name, sir?" the sergeant said,

pausing in front of me; and I took out my card-case.

" My card," said I.

" Remember, my friend has made no attempt to avoid arrest: this is Florence Burke, commonly called Lord Kilmorna," said Foster.

" The name here is Terence," the sergeant said.

"Then your warrant must be for somebody else," said I.

"Florence is a girl's name," said the sergeant wisely, "and it is very like Terence."

"Let us go back again to the cabin." said Kitty to Foster, and at this the sergeant turned round and peered at her.

"You know me, I daresay," she said loftily.

On Board the "Iniquity"

"Certainly, ma'am — Madame Moroni," he said abruptly, and held the card to the lantern.

"Lord Kilmorna it is!" said a familiar voice in the background, and I saw John Peter Maclean among the other policemen. "I know him well," he went on; "does n't he live in my mother's house in the Temple?"

The other policemen came up and reported they had found no one suspicious; so the sergeant, laying his hand on my left shoulder, said something or other; but I am not sure what it was, for though the arrest could mean nothing, and I had expected it, yet, when it came, I was so taken aback and unpleasantly thrilled, I lost my head for a minute. All I know is, he did not exclaim in an echoing voice, "I arrest you in the

name of the Queen!" as he would have done
in a play; and I rather think what he said
was, "Come along with me, please," and I
was half-way across the gangway, and was
dimly aware the police were surprised to
see my stature diminished, when one said,
"And are you coming ashore, ma'am?"

At this it struck me she must come with
me now, since she would have certainly
landed with Terence, and I knew the policemen had a doubt, as it was.

"May I help you?" said I, holding my
hand out; and she came.

"I'll be with you in a little," said
Foster. "There is some silly mistake, of
course, and I must see about bail."

The tug started for shore, and the "Iniquity" was dim in the mist. A cry came over
the water, "Kitty, Kitty! come back!" I

thought she would have cried out answering, but I whispered, "No, no!"

We stood face to face: and that voice echoed in the dusk and the distance. Then she sank down on the seat, and hid her face in her hands.

CHAPTER V

IN THE HANDS OF POLICE

SO the tug reached the Surrey side: and we landed, and went across, in the snow, to a little house by the River. There Kitty and I were shown into a parlour, where everything was neat and uncomfortable; while the others went into another room, and reported their return and success. Because the door was open, I heard them talking to some one, who did not seem overjoyed at their tidings, but said, "Bring him in," as if the affair was a nuisance. So I was asked into the other room, and had hardly crossed the threshold before a man there, at a long table, exclaimed, "That's not the fellow we wanted."

"What?" cried the sergeant.

"I know this boy well enough," said the man at the table, a precise fellow, with cropped hair and a natty beard and a mechanical way.

"Sir!" I broke in, stung by the word " boy," but the sergeant said hurriedly, —

"His friends said he was Lord Kilmorna, sir, and so did Maclean."

"Maclean!" said the other indignantly, as if he was glad of an excuse to be savage, "and what has he got to do with it?"

"But I assure you it's Lord Kilmorna," said Constable John Peter Maclean, almost in tears. "I tell you he lives in my mother's house in the Temple."

A Child in the Temple

"Of all the mutton-headed muddling irrepressible idiots!" said the man at the
table.

"Tell me, what have I done now?" sobbed
Maclean.

"You stupid owl! you have arrested the
wrong man," said the sergeant.

"I'll leave London to-morrow!" mur-
mured John Peter, in a tone of despair.

"A word with you, Mr. Burke," said the
man at the table, and all the others went
out.

"Look here, sir," said he, "you have
assisted a criminal."

"What criminal?" said I loftily.

"But between you and me," he said, "you
have done us a service."

"What do you mean?"

"Yes," said he; "that cousin of yours is

either a fool or a lunatic, or both, and we are glad to be rid of him."

"You tried to keep him."

"Reluctantly," said he. "His friends in a certain Society were denouncing him daily."

"But why?"

"Because his trial would advertise them," said he; "and they disliked him sincerely, for he treated the whole thing as a farce."

"He is too humorous for London," said I.

"We agree with you there," he answered, "and we frightened him out of it. There is no harm in his craziness: who knows but it will be welcomed in Paris?"

"Then why did you stop the launch?" I said doubtingly.

"We had to," said he. "They had just sent us all the details about it; but I had chosen the dullest sergeant I knew.   I speak plain, Mr. Burke; for I want you to keep your cousin abroad."

"I can't interfere," said I.

"You might give him a hint," said he. "If he comes back, he'll be arrested at once, for we are tired of his playfulness. Good-night, Mr. Burke."

The sergeant had a cab at the door: it was a hansom, and the driver, a burly and short fellow, appeared to have been remembering Christmas.

As I helped Kitty in, and then gave him her address in the Haymarket, and got in myself, I heard Maclean say, "I am leaving England, my lord."

I had heard that before, so I said absently, "Good-bye, and good luck."

In the Hands of Police

"Good-bye, your lordship. It is all very well for you to live here, but I am better away; London is no place for an honest man," he said, sighing.

Kitty was silent and tragical, in a struggle with tears. When the light of a lamp was on her face, she was woe-begone; and after I told her Terence was not in danger, we hardly opened our lips, but sat there side by side, in the hurrying hansom, as the horse sped through the snowy forsaken streets by the water, and then floundered and slipped in the mud and slush of the highways, where the people were out. There the shops were ablaze, and the costers' barrows were dazzling the customers with flares, and the crowds were clamorous with shouting and songs. So we went over the black river and through the silent roads in the City, and the clatter of Cheapside, and where the hulk of Saint Paul's lifted a white dome in the dark.

"I'll put you down at the Temple," said Kitty to me, as we were coming to Fleet Street.

"Won't you let me see you safe home?" said I.

"No, thank you," she said. "And we'll be passing your gate. Guess what I've been thinking about."

"What?"

"Kilmorna, and old days at the Farm," said she.

"Good days," said I.

"I was near calling you 'Master Larry' when I spoke to you now. Miss Curly and you were kind to us — I haven't forgotten. You were a little king in my eyes: I prayed for you at morning and night. A minute ago, we passed a fellow that knew you, and I saw his astonishment. What will become of your reputation, my dear?"

But I did not answer, for I was thinking of Curly.

"Look here," she went on, with her mocking lightness, instead of that unusual gravity, "do you still say your prayers, child?"

"Of course," I said, in embarrassment.

"Every night and morning?"

"Of course," I said again, and I reddened.

"Oh, Lord!" she said, laughing, "and you live in the Temple! What a pretty blush you have still! Sweet little saint! Does it kneel down by its tiny bed in its little white nightshirt?"

"Here we are at the gate," said I, glad of

the chance to reach up to the trap-door in the roof of the hansom and tell the driver to stop.

"Bless its little heart! Is it cross?" she said, laughing; and then, suddenly grave, and touching my sleeve, she went on, "Look here — you must n't mind me — I don't mean it — will you promise to pray for me?"

"For you?" I said.

"Do you think I am past praying for?"

"Of course I will, if you want it," said I, more and more confused; and I got out of the hansom, and stood there by the step.

"I want it badly," she said, sobbing, and leant back in the corner, and put her hands to her face.

I did not know in the least what I should answer or do.

"Why are you standing there like a

ninny?" she cried, sitting up, and facing me suddenly. "Why don't you tell that damned fool of a cabman to drive me home to the Haymarket?"

The porter let me in at the wicket-gate, and he appeared to be shocked to see me gadding with such a pretty companion. After all, it was no business of his, said I to myself, sullenly, as I went down the Lane; and still, for all that, his look made me wretched, as my happiest moods can be dashed by a look from a stranger or a glance from a cab-horse. Any sensitive rider might be depressed by a hostile look from an animal he was going to mount; but I knew it was weak to mind the thoughts of a horse seen passing by in the Strand. Time and again I have told myself it is vanity makes me want to like all, and have the friendship of every one, and daily I come across people it is hard to appreciate; but that softness of mine weakens me in spite of my age.

Now I had gone by Brick Court before it dawned on me the porter's reproachful air was meant to be humorous, and this took such a weight from my heart, I had a mind to go back, and wish him a merry Christmas, and double the tip he had already received; but resisting this temptation, I reached Plowden Buildings, and then there was a skurry of paws and the clattering of a chain, and that criminal Mab was making wildly to meet me, as if she was beginning to fear I was not coming at all.

"Mab," said I, as I let myself into my black rooms, "you will be sorry to hear your

master has been making a fool of himself."
At this she began gnawing my trousers, to
show she was not surprised and was affectionate still. "It was not for the first time,"
I went on, "and I don't think it will be
for the last, unless his character changes.
Character never really changes," I said, as
I tumbled over a chair. "Though time may
teach me hypocrisy, I can never do more
than make believe to be rational."

By the time I had lit the lamp and the
fire, I remembered I had gone without dinner, and lacking the energy to order it now,
I determined to make a meal of sardines.
But when I sought them, I found only a card
of Foster's, with the words, "I have eaten
the sardines as a Christmas-box."

"Have you dined," said I, "animal?"
and her philosophical look told me she had;

and I discovered a flask of Chianti and some
biscuits remaining in the tin box of the
Kilmorna Estate, and was content with that
fare. So I gathered several volumes from
my shelves, and piled them up on my table,
to save myself the trouble of rising, if I
should tire of a book when I had settled
down to be quiet. Then I laid the cigarettes and the matches and a glass within
reach, and so went to my bedroom, and got
into evening dress, and then sighed with
relief to find myself enabled to dream instead
of taking a part in the long hurry of London.

" Do you want to break my heart with your
wilfulness?" said I, as I saw my comrade at
her ease in the fender.

"Do leave me alone," she said drowsily,
in the language of tails.

"If you don't come out of that in a minute,

I 'll be throwing a book at you," I went on, with an increased indignation.

At this she glanced at the books, to see whether they were borrowed; but noticing only mine on the table, she laid her head on her paws with a contemplative sigh.

Touched by her happy look, I relented. "Well, after all," said I, "Christmas only comes once a year, — a good thing for fellows that live alone in the Temple, — and I am going to bed soon, so you may as well be enjoying yourself just as you like. I 'll have to rub you down with your clothes-brush with an unusual care, and wrap you tight in your tennis-shirt and blanket, before I can let you sleep in the bed; — but you have brought that on yourself."

Again she sighed, as much as to say it

A Child in the Temple

was worth it; and so I filled a glass with Chianti.

"Child," said I to her, "a glass of Chianti won't do you any harm, I am sure, because, of course, you 'll have none."

At this I drank her health, with respect, and dined off biscuits, and, lighting a cigarette, took up Forster's "Goldsmith," and was soon in my grief. I did not live in those days when I might have been Oliver's Boswell and the friend of his loneliness. But the writer's name kept reminding me of my friend on the launch.

Foster — I thought — does not understand me at all. I remember his scorn when he found me tying a green bow on Mab's tail on St. Patrick's morning, while the creature herself regarded me with a tolerant smile, as if she said, "Do you expect me to wear that, out of doors?" And he called me a baby when I bought her a coat; but when she and I went to feed the gulls driven up the Thames by the frost, she was so proud of her dress I did not mind if all creation was grinning. "Brother," the gulls cried, "come away! You have been cheated enough by unemotional cockneys;" and Mab, under my arm, barked at them like a monster, though here she is as still as if my chambers were haunted by the ghost of a dog.

Strange a small dog should understand me so well when a wise Londoner fails. She and I fell in love at first sight, for I was moping along St. Martin's Lane on a savage evening last winter, when a very small pup, in a cage by a dog-fancier's door, jumped at her bars and whimpered, "Take me home with you, Larry! 'T is a good world — and

A Child in the Temple

I have been put here by mistake." The only
time she is puzzled is when I get up in the
night because I have forgotten to cover the
window-sills with crumbs for the sparrows.

Curly Adair used to find me easy to know.
We were not clever enough to misunderstand
one another. Our souls were knit when we
were children, and we trusted to Love's un-
reasoning insight instead of cynical wisdom.
Certain it is, she does not claim to be clever,
— though she is as wholesome as sweet, and
by very much more handsome than fine, —
but that makes her the more fitted for me,
a man moonstruck and extremely unwise and
only learned enough to make my ignorance
scandalous. Now she has chosen to give her
life to the poor. She might have thought of
me first; for, goodness knows, I am poor
enough. I can go on quietly here, for to-

In the Hands of Police

day I had my fill of adventures: I have sown my wild oats, and I settle to a respectable life.

Well, it is something to be one of the last men in the Temple; for the Benchers are destroying the old place, and it will soon be a name. Lodgings too fine for the small purses of students will have the place of the garrets of the men of the past. Sometimes I amuse myself thinking how many lads have come up from colleges or homes in the country to find their destiny here. What a woeful array of prodigals has turned to repentance! Those were good days for them: now it is the custom to let the calf fatten and put the knife in the prodigal. How many thousands of surly old fellows have looked up from their books to see Death tapping with skeleton fingers on the pane in the fog!

A Child in the Temple

Foster tells me a horn is blown daily to summon the students from hunting the hares on the other side of the River. Now we hunt the wild- goose, — what horn shall summon us back from those adventurous chases? The old Templars lie in the round church of the Knights, and the young ones in the neighbouring Law Courts. Remembrances of the Wars of the Roses, and Elizabeth, and the Fire, and the Plague, and other pleasanter things, will be abandoned to books. Would you rather be connected with Shakspere or a drain? — it is a matter of taste.

At this point, I was startled by a knock at the door.

Because it is well known in the Temple a man is not "at home" when the outer door of his chambers is shut, I was wondering who could be rude enough to break in upon my privacy now, as I got up from my chair. As I opened the door, I saw the drowsy and red face of the cabman who had driven me home, and I was afraid some accident had happened to Kitty.

" Well, what do you want? " said I.

" Are you the gent wot I druv to the Temple Gite with a lydy? " said he sleepily.

" Yes — what is it? "

" That porter, 'e gave me yer address."

" Well? "

" Says you to me — ' Aymarket.' Says I to you, ' Right y' are, Guvnor ! ' Says that little lydy, as I were a-drivin' along, — ' Waterloo Bridge.' "

" What is all this about? " said I, crossly. " I paid you more than enough."

" Says I to myself, ' That little bloke ' —

beg yer pardon, Guvnor — 'that gent 'e paid me my fare, an' few of them does — so I am blawsted,' says I, ' if I don't tell 'im 'is gal 'as gone an' drownded 'erself.' "

" Good God ! " I cried, horror-struck.

" Pore thing ! an' she so young ! " he said, sobbing.

" The man has been drinking," I thought. " The thing is impossible."

" Tell me what occurred," said I quietly.

" Says I to the copper wot walks about on the bridge, ' I 'ave a soft 'art,' says I. ' You 'ave a soft 'ed,' says 'e, an' that young copper 'e lawfed. Says I, 'I caw n't bear to see that little lydy a-drownin'.' ' Then wy are you wytin?' he says, lawfin' again."

" Has anything happened?" said I, impatiently.

" Hanythin' 'appened?" said the cabman,

indignantly, " hain't I told you that gal were stawndin' there on the bridge, a-lookin' down at the water? "

" And what then? "

" ' She's a-goin' to jump hoff,' says I to the copper, and says he, ' You are goin' to drive hoff, an' pretty quick too: I won't stawnd none o' yer foolin'.' Says I to myself, ' I 'll go to that bleedin' little ' — beg pardon, Guvnor — ' that 'ere little gent, an' tell 'im 'is gal 'as drownded 'erself, and wish 'im a merry Christmas, an' maybe — ' "

" Here you are," said I, and gave him a shilling, and shut the door in his face.

Going back to my room, I stood looking down at the fire a minute in doubt, since, though the cabman appeared to have taken more than was needful, his story made me uneasy, for Kitty's manner was strange when

we parted, and as I remembered her talk of
my prayers, I was embarrassed again. My
heart smote me, as if I should have seen to
her, and I fancied her standing there on that
dark bridge where so many had found an
end to their sorrows. Then I thought of
her kneeling in that dim chapel, and remembered her troubled air on the launch, and it
seemed to me now I understood her at last.

Anyway, I could drive to the bridge and
then to her rooms, and so make sure she was
back. With that I put on my coat — to
Mab's unbounded astonishment — and turned
down the lights, and led her out of the
chambers. This time she did not drag at
her chain, as she mostly did, but came
pattering along at my side, as if she walked
in a dream. As I went down, I could hear
shriekings of " Murder! Police! " by the

door: and I thought it was the voice of the cabman.

All was silent again as I came to the ground floor, but I fancied Maclean was a little more breathless than usual, as I gave him the dog.

"Your lordship was disturbed by the noise?" he gasped.

"Not at all. What was it?" said I.

"It was the cabman: he said you had a hard heart," said Maclean.

"Well," said I, "take care of the dog, and I'll be back in an hour." But that promise was rash, as I found out before long.

CHAPTER VI

AT THE GATE OF THE CONVENT

THE snow shone like a river between the menacing walls. Here and there it gleamed on a sill where there was light in a window; but most the houses were black, as the men had gone away to the country.

I stepped out into the rush of the Strand: even at that hour there were many people abroad. Leaving the Temple's solitude made me feel as if I came from a prison: and I was glad to be out, as if tragedy ceased to be possible in prosy surroundings.

So I signed to a hansom, and got into it, and said "Waterloo Bridge" to the driver, a

At the Gate of the Convent

thin boy with a cough. We passed those hypocritical Law Courts, more like a cathedral than ever in the moonlight and snow, and the churches of St. Clement Danes and St. Mary-le-Strand: but beyond Somerset House there was the usual block, where a constable stood under the lamp in the street to keep the drivers in order.

At the near end of the bridge I got out of the cab, and, accosting a stiff constable, asked had there been an accident lately.

"Accident?" said he sternly, "wot accident?"

"Well," said I, airily, with a show of indifference, "I mean has — that is — did any one fall in the river?"

"Three," said he solemnly.

"Three!" I cried, trembling, with all my fears coming back.

A Child in the Temple

"Lawst week," he went on.

"I mean to-night."

"But you said litely," said he.

"Has any one jumped into the river to-night," I asked earnestly: and his stoical countenance altered a little, as if something was beginning to dawn on him.

Said he gloomily, "Might you be hawskin' about a beautiful gal?"

"Yes, yes."

"Wot was in furs?" he went on.

"The very one."

"Hand wot comes up in an 'ansom, hand 'ad been givin' the cabby too many drinks on the wy?"

"Yes! yes! the same," I cried, though neither Kitty nor I had anything to do with the drinks.

The policeman turned his back on me

suddenly, and looked away up the River; and then in the words of the cabman, "that young copper 'e lawfed."

That laugh was so loud and abrupt, and so unprovoked by my tragical errand, that I believed he was mad; but he turned back to me, looking as stiff and solemn as ever.

"Young gent," said he sadly, "I 've seen more of the world, so you 'll excuse me if I speak like a fawther. It was crool of you not to have given that gal hall she could have possibly hawsked. I dessay now 't was a troifle like a necklice of diamonds that made you quarrel to-noight. Now that I 'ave seen you, young gent, I can quoite hunderstawnd 'ow hany lydy would tell you she 'd jump into the Thames."

Drawing myself up to my full height, I

gave him a scowl, — though I felt it was wasted, for he was incredibly big.

"Then she has gone away?" I said sternly.

"She 'ave gone awy," he said stolidly.

"Where?" said I.

"'ome," said he. "'Aymarket. I 'eard 'er tellin' a cabby."

As I turned away he went on:

"When you want a gal to do you credit by drownin' 'erself for yer sake, you should n't give her such clothes; for 'ow could she be so 'ard-'arted as to be spilin' those furs? There's more come to the bridge than will jump into the River," he said sadly, as I got in the cab. "You my bring a gal to the water, but you cawn't mike her jump."

"Where to, sir?" said the driver.

"Haymarket," said I, blushing.

At the Gate of the Convent

The policeman turned his back quickly; and as I drove off, I heard him laughing again.

As I drove to the Haymarket, I was beginning to wonder what I should do if Kitty proved to be there. I decided to inquire at the door, and make a rapid escape. Of course, a couple of fellows I knew went by in a hansom as I was pulling her bell, and I saw them grinning, delighted. Her man said she had gone out after lunch, and he did not seem to suppose she was coming back till the morrow; and he was calm and discreet.

"Big Ben" was drowsily striking eleven, as I stood there in the snow. My uneasiness came back, and as now I had taken so much trouble already, I felt inclined to do more; so as I got into the hansom, I said "Jerusalem House."

A Child in the Temple

"'Ammersmith?" said the lad, and I nodded; and then as we passed down Piccadilly, I kept thinking of what she said at the door of the chapel, and I was hopeful of finding her safe with her sister at the convent, and so I lounged in a corner, and was contented enough. Even the thought of my letter to Curly did not trouble me much; that was past praying for, now, and I was pleasantly tired.

A little after the spot where the Green Park begins on the left, there is a place where, at night, the long thoroughfare has the look of a hill; and the lamps seem to wane on that slope, and almost touch in the distance. For some reason or other, I love that sight, and it gives me a thrill of romance, as if that avenue led to an adventurous kingdom. Driving to prosy dinners and hot

At the Gate of the Convent

dances in Kensington, and certain of finding them as much alike as the strips of carpet outside, I have that stirring minute as if my life was to turn fortunate from the work of a moment. Now that thrill startled me with a stronger insistence and an irrational hope.

As we went along Brompton, and then a little beyond the Oratory, turned into the Fulham Road and by the Boltons to West Kensington, the sidewalks became dispeopled and dark, and we were in streets where there was snow on the ground, and passers were rare, and only curtainless windows or public-houses at corners enlivened the monotonous walls. At times I would catch glimpses of fellows standing before the bars of the public-houses, and joining feebly and bashfully in a music-hall chorus. At other times I would see people assembled in parlours, where holly and the mistletoe hung. More than once I caught sight of a shadowed face at a window, watching for some one, as I went by in the dark. There were others about in the snowy dusk of the streets, — men and women who slunk with the dogged and lagging tread of the homeless, looking sideways at doorsteps, as if they were longing to lie down for a little till the policemen set them moving again, — and girls with a jaunty bearing and extravagant rags.

Off and on, in the quiet places, I heard the hacking cough of the driver, and I thought of him perched up on the hansom all the night, plying for fares, and going back to his bed in a slum, in the grey of the morning, with but little or nothing for the hire of the cab. Then I thought of Curly Adair in the chill convent, surrendering her youth as a sacrifice for the sake of the poor. With these thoughts, my own life in my dark rooms at the top of an old house in the Temple appeared to grow scandalous with iniquitous luxury, and I was full of remorse because I revelled alone on sardines and an occasional cutlet. So it was in a doleful mood of repentance I arrived finally at Jerusalem House.

The convent was hidden behind a wall on the left of a white and desolate road. A woman was kneeling beside the door in the wall. The moon was on her, and made her shadow black on the snow.

Stopping the hansom, I went up to her, and saw it was Kitty. She knelt there with clasped hands, and cried out in a low voice, and despairingly, as if she knew it was vain:

A Child in the Temple

" Let me in ! Let me in ! Sister Mercy."

Standing on her left, I perceived the door was shut, but a little grating was open, and a nun's face was beyond it, and shadowed so much I could hardly see it at all.

" I can't let you in," the nun whispered, and I thought she was crying. "It is too late ; and you must come in the morning — "

But Kitty cried out again so woefully, it hurt me to hear her, "Let me in ! Let me in ! Sister Mercy ! "

" Kitty, darlin'," the nun answered her, " I can't let you in."

" I have a cab here," I said softly. "Won't you come away now ? It 's against their rules to let any one in, you know, so late in the night."

" You ! " she cried, starting up faintly, and leaning her right hand on the door. " How did you find me? This is my home now, and I shall not go away."

"Really, you must come," I said; and as I was speaking the door was flung open, and a cab was behind me.

"She shall not go," cried Curly, there on the threshold. "Dearest, it is never too late," she went on, and flung her arms around Kitty and drew her into the convent.

Kitty lay in her arms as a child clings to its mother.

"And you," Curly cried, looking down at me with sad and rebuking eyes, "you shall not trouble her here."

My brain reeled to think Curly believed I was trying to mislead Kitty Moroney. Then some one threw me aside, and a big fellow sprang forward, attempting to draw Kitty away.

A Child in the Temple

"Kitty, don't abandon me! Kitty," he cried.

"Terence!" she said.

"Terence!" I gasped.

"Lord Kilmorna!" cried Curly, as if she thought him a ghost; and she drew back, and Kitty stood there between them.

"Kitty dear, come with me!" he said.

"Never!" she sobbed. "Dear, you must not see me again."

"But you love me?" he cried.

"With all my heart; and yet, it is good-bye now between us."

"Kitty," he cried. "I want you to marry me. We'll help one another to begin a new life without a thought of the past."

"Oh, how could I, Terence?" she said, trembling. "Your friends —"

At the Gate of the Convent

" My friends are few, and have great hearts,"
he broke in.

" I mean London — " she said.

"I am leaving it for ever to-morrow,"
said he.

"Oh, you are in danger!" she cried, with
a sudden thought of his risk.

"No, I have set that right," he replied.
"We will be married to-morrow and go away
to the South."

"If it could be so!" she said, crying.

"It shall be so," he said firmly.

"Who am I that you should make me your
wife?" she said. "You must marry a good
girl, and forget —"

"Stop!" he cried. "You must n't say
such things, Kitty. Who am I that I should
fancy you love me?"

"God knows I do," she said.

A Child in the Temple

" Then you will forgive me," said he.

"You have always been kindness itself," she said. "And no matter whether you were or not, I only want to be with you. Oh, if I only knew what was right!"

" If you love him, your place is with him," said Curly.

" Oh, Sister," sobbed Kitty, " I owe my life to God as a penitent."

"We all owe Him our lives, dear," said Curly, gently: " but you can give Him your life as well in the world as in the peace of a convent. You may be turning your back on the work He wants you to do. Why should you think He would set lovers asunder?"

" Hear! hear!" I cried frantically, carried away by excitement and my delighted surprise at finding Curly so sensible.

" Oh, you 're there, are you?" said Terence

with a laugh of relief, as if he was glad I broke in on that emotional strain.

"Kitty," he went on, flinging his left arm round my neck and lugging me forward. "My whole family is here, to tell you it consents to our marriage."

"It does, indeed — with a full heart!" I cried wildly.

Kitty looked at me for a moment with eyes wavering between laughing and tears. Then she held out her hand to me.

"God bless you, Master Larry," said she; but before I could take it, Terence caught hold of it, nearly flinging me prone, and he went down on his knee.

"It is mine!" said he, raising her little hand to his lips.

"It will be yours to-morrow," said Curly, laughing a little, and drew Kitty away, — and

A Child in the Temple

Terence and I were standing out in the cold.

I stared at the door, with a sudden chill at my heart. But there was no chill about Terence, as he caught me by the shoulders and shook me, by way of expressing his relief and content.

"Larry, dear heart, you are a blessing disguised as a little nuisance," he said. "Oh, Larry, darling, how I wish I could find some one to fight!"

"But how did you get here?" said I, breathless.

"Through you — you delightful little duffer!" he cried, letting me go.

"How's that?" said I.

"Her servant heard you directing your cabman. I would never have thought of it!"

"But the police?"

At the Gate of the Convent

" I tell you, child, I love that inspector."

" Why, what did he do ? "

" When I found Kitty was gone, I came ashore, for I would n't have her suffer annoyance for helping me to escape. ' Don't tell me your name,' said the inspector. ' Sir, I will, if I choose,' said I sternly. ' Listen ! ' said he, ' two young people were here just now and have gone home to the Haymarket.' ' Both ? ' I said jealously. ' Well, they started together,' said he, grinning. ' A launch on the River was searched to-night, and so we won't interfere with it, if it travels to-morrow.' ' I see,' said I, ' but after to-morrow ? ' ' We 'll have to search it again. Good-night,' said he — and so I am here."

With that he turned to his hansom.

" Can I give you a lift ? " said he.

" Thanks. I have a cab over there," said I.

A Child in the Temple

"Good-bye, Larry," said he, wringing my hand. "By-the-bye, I've made you a present: it is Kilmorna, you know."

"Kilmorna?" said I, not understanding.

"I meant all along to hand it over to you," he said. "The place is no use to me: you know I never go near it. I told the lawyers to send you the deeds on Christmas morning, my son."

"Kilmorna?" I said, incredulous still.

"The old place is yours," he said, "and a rational income to keep it going in comfort. Well, good-bye, and good luck!" and before I could thank him, he leapt into the cab, and shouted some address, and the driver slashed his horse, and they were off at full speed, and I was standing alone.

Half my dreams had come true, when I expected it least: now I could leave London, and be in Ireland again. But I heard of it first by the black doors of the convent where Curly lived as a nun: and so what use was it now?

"Whisper, Larry!" said Curly.

The grating had opened suddenly, and her face was behind it.

" Oh, Curly, is that you?" I cried timidly. " Sister Curly — that is — "

"Not Sister Curly any more," she said, " Larry."

" Oh, what do you mean?" I cried, with a sudden aching of hope, and yet as I spoke I felt my thought was absurd, for she was dressed as a nun, and even now I could see the white band on her forehead beyond the bars of the grating.

"I got your letter to-day. Why did you address it so funnily? But you were always fond of a joke."

A Child in the Temple

"Oh," I cried in despair. "Forgive me! I did n't mean it! It was that horrible dog."

"You did n't mean it?" she said, with pain in her voice.

"Every word of it!" I cried.

"So you knew I was coming out?" she went on. "How did you hear of it? I am only a novice, and I had decided to leave the convent to-morrow: I am not good enough for this life."

"You, not good enough, Curly?"

"The Sisters are angels," she said, "and I am only a girl. So now I shall take care of a sinner."

"A sinner!" I said, in dismay.

"A kindly little sinner," she said. "A merry Christmas!" and then adding some words in a low voice, she shut the grating, as near us the big clock of the convent

At the Gate of the Convent

began striking twelve, and on all the steeples the joy bells began pealing for Christmas.

Those last words she said were " Whisper, Larry, I love you."

SOME PRESS OPINIONS.

THE WOOD OF THE BRAMBLES.

The book displays the vivid descriptive power and rugged strength of a high-pitched and intensely dramatic imagination.
The Times.

The great Irish novel we have all been waiting for.
KATHERINE TYNAN *in Weekly Register.*

One of the quaintest and most delightful of books.
Athenæum.

Bids fair to become a classic. — *Black and White.*

A work which should place the author in the position of *the* Irish novelist of the day. — *Whitehall Review.*

A book which is predestined to fame. It is unfair to class Mr. Mathew as the Kipling or the Barrie of Ireland; his individuality is all his own. — *Vanity Fair.*

This book carries the rare stamp of a temperament. Mr. Mathew brings you a whole world, — the quaint, pathetic, and yet noble and gallant world of Ireland in the last century.
RICHARD LE GALLIENNE *in Idler.*

Whether he be grave or gay, Mr. Mathew has the finely individualized touch which is always rare, and the "Wood of the Brambles" is in consequence a very captivating story.
Daily Chronicle.

AT THE RISING OF THE MOON.

For literary capital, Mr. Frank Mathew has a good deal of mother-wit, with much quiet humour, and a particularly intimate knowledge of his country. Nothing Irish seems alien to him; all the stories are marked by grace and moderation of style. — *Bookman.*

Ireland has found her Kipling. The very heart of Ireland beats in the stories, and every figure abounds with character. — *Boston Herald.*

Mr. Mathew has done for Moher and its people what Mr. Barrie has done for Thrums. All the features of Irish life are portrayed with keen sympathy and loving insight, and the book teems with that apparently unconscious humour which is so racy of the soil. — *Glasgow Herald.*

The delicacy of touch, the purity of diction, and the quiet humour that have placed Mr. Barrie in the position he occupies. There is little of the rollicking Irish humour in these stories, but much that is quaint and subtle. — *Detroit Free Press.*

JOHN LANE

THE
BODLEY
HEAD
VIGO St
W.
Telegrams
BODLEIAN
LONDON"

E·NEW·

CATALOGUE *of* PUBLICATIONS *in* BELLES LETTRES *all at net prices*

List of Books

IN

BELLES LETTRES

Published by John Lane

𝕿𝖍𝖊 𝕭𝖔𝖉𝖑𝖊𝖞 𝕳𝖊𝖆𝖉

VIGO STREET, LONDON, W.

Adams (Francis).
ESSAYS IN MODERNITY. Crown 8vo.
5s. net. [*Shortly.*
A CHILD OF THE AGE. (*See* KEY-
NOTES SERIES.)

A. E.
HOMEWARD SONGS BY THE WAY.
Sq. 16mo, wrappers. 1s. 6d. net.
*Transferred to the present Pub-
lisher.* [*Second Edition.*
THE EARTH BREATH, AND OTHER
POEMS. [*In preparation.*

Aldrich (T. B.)
LATER LYRICS. Sm. Fcap. 8vo.
2s. 6d. net.

Allen (Grant).
THE LOWER SLOPES: A Volume of
Verse. With Title-page and Cover
Design by J. ILLINGWORTH KAY.
Crown 8vo. 5s. net.
THE WOMAN WHO DID. (*See* KEY-
NOTES SERIES.)
THE BRITISH BARBARIANS. (*See*
KEYNOTES SERIES.)

Arcady Library (The).
A Series of Open-Air Books. Edited
by J. S. FLETCHER. With Cover
Designs by PATTEN WILSON.
Each volume crown 8vo. 5s. net.
  I. ROUND ABOUT A BRIGHTON
     COACH OFFICE. By MAUDE
     EGERTON KING. With
     over 30 Illustrations by
     LUCY KEMP-WELCH.
  II. LIFE IN ARCADIA. By J. S.
     FLETCHER. With 20 Illus-
     trations by PATTEN WIL-
     SON.

Arcady Library (The)—*cont.*
  III. SCHOLAR GIPSIES. By JOHN
     BUCHAN. With 7 full-page
     Etchings by D.Y. CAMERON
  IV. IN THE GARDEN OF PEACE.
     By HELEN MILMAN. With
     24 Illustrations by EDMUND
     H. NEW.
  V. THE HAPPY EXILE. By H.
     D. LOWRY. With 6 Etch-
     ings by E. PHILIP PIMLOTT.
     [*In preparation*

Beeching (Rev. H. C.).
IN A GARDEN : Poems. With Title-
page designed by ROGER FRY.
Crown 8vo. 5s. net.
ST. AUGUSTINE AT OSTIA. Crown
8vo, wrappers. 1s. net.

Beerbohm (Max).
THE WORKS OF MAX BEERBOHM.
With a Bibliography by JOHN
LANE. Sq. 16mo. 4s. 6d. net.

Benson (Arthur Christopher)
LYRICS. Fcap. 8vo, buckram. 5s.
net.
LORD VYET AND OTHER POEMS.
Fcap. 8vo. 3s. 6d. net.

**Bodley Head Anthologies
(The).**
Edited by ROBERT H. CASE. With
Title-page and Cover Designs by
WALTER WEST. Each volume
crown 8vo. 5s. net.
  I. ENGLISH EPITHALAMIES.
     By ROBERT H. CASE.

Bodley Head Anthologies (The)—*continued*.

II. MUSA PISCATRIX. By JOHN BUCHAN. With 6 Etchings by E. PHILIP PIMLOTT.

III. ENGLISH ELEGIES. By JOHN C. BAILEY.
[*In preparation.*

IV. ENGLISH SATIRES. By CHAS. HILL DICK.
[*In preparation.*

Bridges (Robert).

SUPPRESSED CHAPTERS AND OTHER BOOKISHNESS. Crown 8vo. 3s. 6d. net. [*Second Edition.*

Brotherton (Mary).

ROSEMARY FOR REMEMBRANCE. With Title-page and Cover Design by WALTER WEST. Fcap. 8vo. 3s. 6d. net.

Crackanthorpe (Hubert).

VIGNETTES. A Miniature Journal of Whim and Sentiment. Fcap. 8vo, boards. 2s. 6d. net.

Crane (Walter).

TOY BOOKS. Re-issue, each with new Cover Design and End Papers. This LITTLE PIG'S PICTURE BOOK, containing:

I. THIS LITTLE PIG.
II. THE FAIRY SHIP.
III. KING LUCKIEBOY'S PARTY.

The three bound in one volume with a decorative cloth cover, end papers, and a newly written and designed preface and title-page. 3s. 6d. net; separately 9d. net each.

MOTHER HUBBARD'S PICTURE BOOK, containing:
I. MOTHER HUBBARD'S.
II. THE THREE BEARS.
III. THE ABSURD A. B. C.

The three bound in one volume with a decorative cloth cover, end papers, and a newly written and designed preface and title-page. 3s. 6d. net; separately 9d. net each.

Custance (Olive).

OPALS: Poems. Fcap. 8vo. 3s. 6d. net.

Dalmon (C. W.).

SONG FAVOURS. With a Title-page by J. P. DONNE. Sq. 16mo. 3s. 6d. net.

Davidson (John).

PLAYS: An Unhistorical Pastoral; A Romantic Farce; Bruce, a Chronicle Play; Smith, a Tragic Farce; Scaramouch in Naxos, a Pantomime. With a Frontispiece and Cover Design by AUBREY BEARDSLEY. Small 4to. 7s. 6d. net.

FLEET STREET ECLOGUES. Fcap. 8vo, buckram. 4s. 6d. net.
[*Third Edition.*

FLEET STREET ECLOGUES. 2nd Series. Fcap. 8vo, buckram. 4s. 6d. net. [*Second Edition.*

A RANDOM ITINERARY AND A BALLAD. With a Frontispiece and Title-page by LAURENCE HOUSMAN. Fcap. 8vo, Irish Linen. 5s. net.

BALLADS AND SONGS. With a Title-page and Cover Design by WALTER WEST. Fcap. 8vo, buckram. 5s. net. [*Fourth Edition.*

NEW BALLADS. Fcap. 8vo, buckram. 4s. 6d. net. [*Second Edition.*

De Tabley (Lord).

POEMS, DRAMATIC AND LYRICAL. By JOHN LEICESTER WARREN (Lord de Tabley). Illustrations and Cover Design by C. S. RICKETTS. Crown 8vo. 7s. 6d. net. [*Third Edition.*

POEMS, DRAMATIC AND LYRICAL. Second Series, uniform in binding with the former volume. Crown 8vo. 5s. net.

Duer (Caroline, and Alice).

POEMS. Fcap. 8vo. 3s. 6d. net.

Egerton (George)

KEYNOTES. (*See* KEYNOTES SERIES.)

DISCORDS. (*See* KEYNOTES SERIES.)

YOUNG OFEG'S DITTIES. A translation from the Swedish of OLA HANSSON. With Title-page and Cover Design by AUBREY BEARDSLEY. Crown 8vo. 3s. 6d. net.

SYMPHONIES. [*In preparation.*

Eglinton (John).

TWO ESSAYS ON THE REMNANT. Post 8vo, wrappers. 1s. 6d. net. *Transferred to the present Publisher.* [*Second Edition.*

Eve's Library.

Each volume, crown 8vo. 3s. 6d. net.

I. MODERN WOMEN. An English rendering of LAURA MARHOLM HANSSON'S "DAS BUCH DER FRAUEN" by HERMIONE RAMSDEN. Subjects: Sonia Kovalevsky, George Egerton, Eleanora Duse, Amalie Skram, Marie Bashkirtseff, A. Ch. Edgren Leffler.

II. THE ASCENT OF WOMAN. By ROY DEVEREUX.

III. MARRIAGE QUESTIONS IN MODERN FICTION. By ELIZABETH RACHEL CHAFMAN.

Fea (Allan).

THE FLIGHT OF THE KING : a full, true, and particular account of the escape of His Most Sacred Majesty King Charles II. after the Battle of Worcester, with Sixteen Portraits in Photogravure and nearly 100 other Illustrations. Demy 8vo. 21s. net.

Field (Eugene).

THE LOVE AFFAIRS OF A BIBLIOMANIAC. Post 8vo. 3s. 6d. net.

Fletcher (J. S.).

THE WONDERFUL WAPENTAKE. By "A SON OF THE SOIL." With 18 full-page Illustrations by J. A. SYMINGTON. Crown 8vo. 5s. 6d. net.

LIFE IN ARCADIA. (*See* ARCADY LIBRARY.)

GOD'S FAILURES. (*See* KEYNOTES SERIES.)

BALLADS OF REVOLT. Sq. 32mo. 2s. 6d. net.

Ford (James L.).

THE LITERARY SHOP AND OTHER TALES. Fcap. 8vo. 3s. 6d. net.

Four-and-Sixpenny Novels.

Each volume with Title-page and Cover Design by PATTEN WILSON. Crown 8vo. 4s. 6d. net.

GALLOPING DICK. By H. B. MARRIOTT WATSON.

THE WOOD OF THE BRAMBLES. By FRANK MATHEW.

THE SACRIFICE OF FOOLS. By R. MANIFOLD CRAIG.

A LAWYER'S WIFE. By Sir NEVILL GEARY, Bart. [*Second Edition.*

WEIGHED IN THE BALANCE. By HARRY LANDER.

GLAMOUR. By META ORRED.

PATIENCE SPARHAWK AND HER TIMES. By GERTRUDE ATHERTON.

THE WISE AND THE WAYWARD. By G. S. STREET.

The following are in preparation :

MIDDLE GREYNESS. By A. J. DAWSON.

DERELICTS. By W. J. LOCKE.

THE MARTYR'S BIBLE. By GEORGE FIFTH.

A CELIBATE'S WIFE. By HERBERT FLOWERDEW.

MAX. By JULIAN CROSKEY.

THE MAKING OF A PRIG. By EVELYN SHARP.

THE TREE OF LIFE. By NETTA SYRETT.

CECILIA. By STANLEY V. MAKOWER.

Fuller (H. B.).

THE PUPPET BOOTH. Twelve Plays. Crown 8vo. 4s. 6d. net.

Gale (Norman).

ORCHARD SONGS. With Title-page and Cover Design by J. ILLINGWORTH KAY. Fcap. 8vo, Irish Linen. 5s. net.

Also a Special Edition limited in number on hand-made paper bound in English vellum. £1 1s. net.

Garnett (Richard).

POEMS. With Title-page by J. ILLINGWORTH KAY. Crown 8vo. 5s. net.

DANTE, PETRARCH, CAMOENS, cxxiv Sonnets, rendered in English. With Title-page by PATTEN WILSON. Crown 8vo. 5s. net.

Gibson (Charles Dana).

DRAWINGS : Eighty-Five Large Cartoons. Oblong Folio. 15s. net.

Gibson (Charles Dana)—
continued.
PICTURES OF PEOPLE. Eighty-Five Large Cartoons. Oblong folio. 15s. net.

Gosse (Edmund).
THE LETTERS OF THOMAS LOVELL BEDDOES. Now first edited. Pott 8vo. 5s. net.
Also 25 copies large paper. 12s. 6d. net

Grahame (Kenneth).
PAGAN PAPERS. With Title-page by AUBREY BEARDSLEY. Fcap. 8vo. 5s. net.
[Out of Print at present.
THE GOLDEN AGE. With Cover Design by CHARLES ROBINSON. Crown 8vo. 3s. 6d. net.
[Fifth Edition.

Greene (G. A.).
ITALIAN LYRISTS OF TO-DAY. Translations in the original metres from about thirty-five living Italian poets, with bibliographical and biographical notes. Crown 8vo. 5s. net.

Greenwood (Frederick).
IMAGINATION IN DREAMS. Crown 8vo. 5s. net.

Hake (T. Gordon).
A SELECTION FROM HIS POEMS. Edited by Mrs. MEYNELL. With a Portrait after D. G. ROSSETTI, and a Cover Design by GLEESON WHITE. Crown 8vo. 5s. net.

Hayes (Alfred).
THE VALE OF ARDEN AND OTHER POEMS. With a Title-page and a Cover designed by E. H. NEW. Fcap. 8vo. 3s. 6d. net.
Also 25 copies large paper. 15s. net.

Hazlitt (William).
LIBER AMORIS; OR, THE NEW PYGMALION. Edited, with an Introduction, by RICHARD LE GALLIENNE. To which is added an exact transcript of the original MS., Mrs. Hazlitt's Diary in Scotland, and letters never before published. Portrait after BEWICK, and facsimile letters. 400 Copies only. 4to, 364 pp., buckram. 21s. net.

Heinemann (William).
THE FIRST STEP; A Dramatic Moment. Small 4to. 3s. 6d. net.

Hopper (Nora).
BALLAD IN PROSE. With a Title-page and Cover by WALTER WEST. Sq. 16mo. 5s. net.
UNDER QUICKEN BOUGHS. With Title-page designed by PATTEN WILSON, and Cover designed by ELIZABETH NAYLOR. Crown 8vo. 5s. net.

Housman (Clemence).
THE WERE WOLF. With 6 full-page Illustrations, Title-page, and Cover Design by LAURENCE HOUSMAN. Sq. 16mo. 3s. 6d. net.

Housman (Laurence).
GREEN ARRAS: Poems. With 6 Illustrations, Title-page, Cover Design, and End Papers by the Author. Crown 8vo. 5s. net.
GOOS AND THEIR MAKERS. Crown 8vo, 3s. 6d. net. *[In preparation.*

Irving (Laurence).
GODEFROI AND YOLANDE: A Play. Sm. 4to. 3s. 6d. net.
[In preparation.

James (W. P.)
ROMANTIC PROFESSIONS: A Volume of Essays. With Title-page designed by J. ILLINGWORTH KAY. Crown 8vo. 5s. net.

Johnson (Lionel).
THE ART OF THOMAS HARDY: Six Essays. With Etched Portrait by WM. STRANG, and Bibliography by JOHN LANE. Crown 8vo. 5s. 6d. net. *[Second Edition.*
Also 150 copies, large paper, with proofs of the portrait. £1 1s. net.

Johnson (Pauline).
WHITE WAMPUM: Poems. With a Title-page and Cover Design by E. H. NEW. Crown 8vo. 5s. net.

Johnstone (C. E.).
BALLADS OF BOY AND BEAK. With a Title-page by F. H. TOWNSEND. Sq. 32mo. 2s. net.

Kemble (E. W.)
KEMBLE'S COONS. 30 Drawings of Coloured Children and Southern Scenes. Large 4to. 5s. net.

Keynotes Series.

Each volume with specially-designed Title-page by AUBREY BEARDS-LEY or PATTEN WILSON. Crown 8vo, cloth. 3s. 6d. net.

I. KEYNOTES. By GEORGE EGERTON.
[*Seventh Edition.*

II. THE DANCING FAUN. By FLORENCE FARR.

III. POOR FOLK. Translated from the Russian of F. Dostoievsky by LENA MILMAN. With a Preface by GEORGE MOORE.

IV. A CHILD OF THE AGE. By FRANCIS ADAMS.

V. THE GREAT GOD PAN AND THE INMOST LIGHT. By ARTHUR MACHEN.
[*Second Edition.*

VI. DISCORDS. By GEORGE EGERTON.
[*Fifth Edition.*

VII. PRINCE ZALESKI. By M. P. SHIEL.

VIII. THE WOMAN WHO DID. By GRANT ALLEN.
[*Twenty-second Edition.*

IX. WOMEN'S TRAGEDIES. By H. D. LOWRY.

X. GREY ROSES. By HENRY HARLAND.

XI. AT THE FIRST CORNER AND OTHER STORIES. By H. B. MARRIOTT WATSON.

XII. MONOCHROMES. By ELLA D'ARCY.

XIII. AT THE RELTON ARMS. By EVELYN SHARP.

XIV. THE GIRL FROM THE FARM. By GERTRUDE DIX.
[*Second Edition.*

XV. THE MIRROR OF MUSIC. By STANLEY V. MAKOWER.

XVI. YELLOW AND WHITE. By W. CARLTON DAWE.

XVII. THE MOUNTAIN LOVERS. By FIONA MACLEOD.

XVIII. THE WOMAN WHO DIDN'T. By VICTORIA CROSSE.
[*Third Edition.*

Keynotes Series—*continued.*

XIX. THE THREE IMPOSTORS. By ARTHUR MACHEN.

XX. NOBODY'S FAULT. By NETTA SYRETT.
[*Second Edition.*

XXI. THE BRITISH BARBARIANS. By GRANT ALLEN.
[*Second Edition.*

XXII. IN HOMESPUN. By E. NESBIT.

XXIII. PLATONIC AFFECTIONS. By JOHN SMITH.

XXIV. NETS FOR THE WIND. By UNA TAYLOR.

XXV. WHERE THE ATLANTIC MEETS THE LAND. By CALDWELL LIPSETT.

XXVI. IN SCARLET AND GREY. By FLORENCE HENNIKER. (With THE SPECTRE OF THE REAL by FLORENCE HEN-NIKER and THOMAS HAR-DY.) [*Second Edition.*

XXVII. MARIS STELLA. By MARIE CLOTHILDE BALFOUR.

XXVIII. DAY BOOKS. By MABEL E. WOTTON.

XXIX. SHAPES IN THE FIRE. By M. P. SHIEL.

XXX. UGLY IDOL. By CLAUD NICHOLSON.

XXXI. KAKEMONOS. By W. CARLTON DAWE.

XXXII. GOD'S FAILURES. By J. S. FLETCHER.

XXXIII. MERE SENTIMENT. By A. J. DAWSON.

XXXIV. A DELIVERANCE. By ALLAN MONKHOUSE
[*In preparation.*

Lane's Library.

Each volume crown 8vo. 3s. 6d. net.

I. MARCH HARES. By HAROLD FREDERIC.
[*Second Edition.*

II. THE SENTIMENTAL SEX. By GERTRUDE WARDEN.

III. GOLD. By ANNIE LINDEN.

Lane's Library—*continued.*

The following are in preparation:

   IV. BROKEN AWAY. By BEA-
      TRICE GRIMSHAW.

   V. A MAN FROM THE NORTH.
     By E. A. BENNETT.

   VI. THE DUKE OF LINDEN. By
     JOSEPH F. CHARLES.

Leather (R. K.).

VERSES. 250 copies. Fcap. 8vo.
3s. net. [*Transferred to the
present Publisher.*

Lefroy (Edward Cracroft.)

POEMS. With a Memoir by W. A.
GILL, and a reprint of Mr. J. A.
SYMONDS' Critical Essay on
"Echoes from Theocritus." Cr.
8vo. Photogravure Portrait. 5s.
net.

Le Gallienne (Richard).

PROSE FANCIES. With Portrait of
the Author by WILSON STEER.
Crown 8vo. Purple cloth. 5s.
net.   [*Fourth Edition.*

Also a limited large paper edition.
12s. 6d. net.

THE BOOK BILLS OF NARCISSUS.
An Account rendered by RICHARD
LE GALLIENNE. With a Frontispiece. Crown 8vo, purple cloth.
3s. 6d. net.   [*Third Edition.*
Also 50 copies on large paper. 8vo.
10s. 6d. net.

ROBERT LOUIS STEVENSON, AN
ELEGY, AND OTHER POEMS,
MAINLY PERSONAL. With Etched
Title-page by D. Y. CAMERON.
Crown 8vo, purple cloth. 4s. 6d.
net.
Also 75 copies on large paper. 8vo.
12s. 6d. net.

ENGLISH POEMS. Crown 8vo, purple cloth. 4s. 6d. net.
       [*Fourth Edition, revised.*

GEORGE MEREDITH : Some Char-
acteristics. With a Bibliography
(much enlarged) by JOHN LANE,
portrait, &c. Crown 8vo, purple
cloth. 5s. 6d. net.
         [*Fourth Edition.*

Le Gallienne (Richard)—*continued.*

THE RELIGION OF A LITERARY
MAN. Crown 8vo, purple cloth.
3s. 6d. net.   [*Fifth Thousand.*
Also a special rubricated edition on
hand-made paper. 8vo. 10s. 6d. net.
RETROSPECTIVE REVIEWS, A LITER-
ARY LOG, 1891–1895. 2 vols.
Crown 8vo, purple cloth. 9s.
net.
PROSE FANCIES (Second Series).
Crown 8vo, Purple cloth. 5s. net.
THE QUEST OF THE GOLDEN GIRL.
Crown 8vo. 5s. net.
See also HAZLITT, WALTON and
COTTON.

Lowry (H. D.).

MAKE BELIEVE. Illustrated by
CHARLES ROBINSON. Crown 8vo,
gilt edges or uncut. 5s. net.
WOMEN'S TRAGEDIES. (*See* KEY-
NOTES SERIES).
THE HAPPY EXILE. (*See* ARCADY
LIBRARY).

Lucas (Winifred).

UNITS : Poems. Fcap. 8vo. 3s. 6d.
net.

Lynch (Hannah).

THE GREAT GALEOTO AND FOLLY
OR SAINTLINESS. Two Plays,
from the Spanish of JOSÉ ECHE-
GARAY, with an Introduction.
Small 4to. 5s. 6d. net.

Marzials (Theo.).

THE GALLERY OF PIGEONS AND
OTHER POEMS. Post 8vo. 4s. 6d.
net. [*Transferred to the present
Publisher.*

The Mayfair Set.

Each volume fcap. 8vo. 3s. 6d. net.
   I. THE AUTOBIOGRAPHY OF A
     BOY. Passages selected by
     his friend G. S. STREET.
     With a Title-page designed
     by C. W. FURSE.
           [*Fifth Edition.*
   II. THE JONESES AND THE
     ASTERISKS. A Story in
     Monologue. By GERALD
     CAMPBELL. With a Title-
     page and 6 Illustrations by
     F. H. TOWNSEND.
          [*Second Edition.*

The Mayfair Set—*continued.*

III. SELECT CONVERSATIONS WITH AN UNCLE, NOW EXTINCT. By H. G. WELLS. With a Title-page by F. H. TOWNSEND.

IV. FOR PLAIN WOMEN ONLY. By GEORGE FLEMING. With a Title-page by PATTEN WILSON.

V. THE FEASTS OF AUTOLYCUS : THE DIARY OF A GREEDY WOMAN. Edited by ELIZABETH ROBINS PENNELL. With a Title-page by PATTEN WILSON.

VI. MRS. ALBERT GRUNDY : OBSERVATIONS IN PHILISTIA. By HAROLD FREDERIC. With a Title-page by PATTEN WILSON. [*Second Edition.*

Meredith (George).

THE FIRST PUBLISHED PORTRAIT OF THIS AUTHOR, engraved on the wood by W. BISCOMBE GARDNER, after the painting by G. F. WATTS. Proof copies on Japanese vellum, signed by painter and engraver. £1 1s. net.

Meynell (Mrs.).

POEMS. Fcap. 8vo. 3s. 6d. net. [*Fifth Edition.*

THE RHYTHM OF LIFE AND OTHER ESSAYS. Fcap. 8vo. 3s. 6d. net. [*Fifth Edition.*

THE COLOUR OF LIFE AND OTHER ESSAYS. Fcap 8vo. 3s. 6d. net. [*Fifth Edition.*

THE CHILDREN. Fcap. 8vo. 3s. 6d. net. [*Second Edition.*

Miller (Joaquin).

THE BUILDING OF THE CITY BEAUTIFUL. Fcap. 8vo. With a Decorated Cover. 5s. net.

Money-Coutts (F. B.).

POEMS. With Title-page designed by PATTEN WILSON. Crown 8vo. 3s. 6d. net.

Monkhouse (Allan).

BOOKS AND PLAYS : A Volume of Essays on Meredith, Borrow, Ibsen, and others. Crown 8vo. 5s. net.

A DELIVERANCE. (*See* KEYNOTES SERIES.)

Nesbit (E.).

A POMANDER OF VERSE. With a Title-page and Cover designed by LAURENCE HOUSMAN. Crown 8vo. 5s. net.

IN HOMESPUN. (*See* KEYNOTES SERIES.)

Nettleship (J. T.).

ROBERT BROWNING : Essays and Thoughts. Crown 8vo. 5s. 6d. net. [*Third Edition.*

Noble (Jas. Ashcroft).

THE SONNET IN ENGLAND AND OTHER ESSAYS. Title-page and Cover Design by AUSTIN YOUNG. Crown 8vo. 5s. net.

Also 50 copies large paper 12s. 6d. net

Oppenheim (Michael).

A HISTORY OF THE ADMINISTRATION OF THE ROYAL NAVY, and of Merchant Shipping in relation to the Navy from MDIX to MDCLX, with an introduction treating of the earlier period. With Illustrations. Demy 8vo. 15s. net.

O'Shaughnessy (Arthur).

HIS LIFE AND HIS WORK. With Selections from his Poems. By LOUISE CHANDLER MOULTON. Portrait and Cover Design. Fcap. 8vo. 5s. net.

Oxford Characters.

A series of lithographed portraits by WILL ROTHENSTEIN, with text by F. YORK POWELL and others. 200 copies only, folio, buckram. £3 3s. net.

25 special large paper copies containing proof impressions of the portraits signed by the artist, £6 6s. net.

Peters (Wm. Theodore).

POSIES OUT OF RINGS. With Title-page by PATTEN WILSON. Sq. 16mo. 2s. 6d. net.

Pierrot's Library.

Each volume with Title-page, Cover and End Papers, designed by AUBREY BEARDSLEY. Sq. 16mo. 2s. net.

   I. PIERROT. By H. DE VERE STACPOOLE.
   II. MY LITTLE LADY ANNE. By MRS. EGERTON CASTLE.
   III. SIMPLICITY. By A. T. G. PRICE.
   IV. MY BROTHER. By VINCENT BROWN.

The following are in preparation :

   V. DEATH, THE KNIGHT, AND THE LADY. By H. DE VERE STACPOOLE.
   VI. MR. PASSINGHAM. By THOMAS COBB.
   VII. TWO IN CAPTIVITY. By VINCENT BROWN.

Plarr (Victor).

IN THE DORIAN MOOD : Poems. With Title-page by PATTEN WILSON. Crown 8vo. 5s. net.

Posters in Miniature : over

250 reproductions of French, English and American Posters with Introduction by EDWARD PENFIELD. Large crown 8vo. 5s. net.

Radford (Dollie).

SONGS AND OTHER VERSES. With a Title-page by PATTEN WILSON. Fcap. 8vo. 4s. 6d. net.

Rhys (Ernest).

A LONDON ROSE AND OTHER RHYMES. With Title-page designed by SELWYN IMAGE. Crown 8vo. 5s. net.

Robertson (John M.).

ESSAYS TOWARDS A CRITICAL METHOD. (New Series) Crown 8vo. 5s. net. [*In preparation.*

St. Cyres (Lord).

THE LITTLE FLOWERS OF ST. FRANCIS: A new rendering into English of the Fioretti di San Francesco. Crown 8vo. 5s. net. (*In preparation.*

Seaman (Owen).

THE BATTLE OF THE BAYS. Fcap. 8vo. 3s. 6d. net.

Sedgwick (Jane Minot).

SONGS FROM THE GREEK. Fcap. 8vo. 3s. 6d. net.

Setoun (Gabriel).

THE CHILD WORLD : Poems. With over 200 Illustrations by CHARLES ROBINSON. Crown 8vo, gilt edges or uncut. 5s. net.

Sharp (Evelyn).

WYMPS : Fairy Tales. With Coloured Illustrations by MABEL DEARMER. Small 4to, decorated cover. 4s. 6d. net.

AT THE RELTON ARMS. (*See* KEYNOTES SERIES.)

THE MAKING OF A PRIG. (*See* FOUR-AND-SIXPENNY NOVELS.)

Shore (Louisa).

POEMS. With an appreciation by FREDERIC HARRISON and a Portrait. Fcap. 8vo. 5s. net.

Short Stories Series.

Each volume Post 8vo. Coloured edges. 2s. 6d. net.

   I SOME WHIMS OF FATE. By MÉNIE MURIEL DOWIE.
   II. THE SENTIMENTAL VIKINGS. By R. V. RISLEY.
   III. SHADOWS OF LIFE. By MRS. MURRAY HICKSON.

Stevenson (Robert Louis).

PRINCE OTTO. A Rendering in French by EGERTON CASTLE. With Frontispiece, Title-page, and Cover Design by D. Y. CAMERON. Crown 8vo. 7s. 6d. net.

Also 50 copies on large paper, uniform in size with the Edinburgh Edition of the Works.

A CHILD'S GARDEN OF VERSES. With over 150 Illustrations by CHARLES ROBINSON. Crown 8vo. 5s. net.   [*Second Edition.*

Stimson (F. J.)

KING NOANETT. A Romance of Devonshire Settlers in New England. Illustrated. Large crown 8vo. 5s. net.

Stoddart (Thos. Tod).

THE DEATH WAKE. With an Introduction by ANDREW LANG. Fcap. 8vo. 5s. net.

Street (G. S.).

EPISODES. Post 8vo. 3s. net.

MINIATURES AND MOODS. Fcap. 8vo. 3s. net. [*Both transferred to the present Publisher.*

QUALES EGO: A FEW REMARKS, IN PARTICULAR AND AT LARGE. Fcap. 8vo. 3s. 6d. net.

THE AUTOBIOGRAPHY OF A BOY. (*See* MAYFAIR SET.)

THE WISE AND THE WAYWARD. (*See* FOUR - AND - SIXPENNY NOVELS.)

Swettenham (F. A.)

MALAY SKETCHES. With a Title-page and Cover Design by PATTEN WILSON. Crown 8vo. 5s. net. [*Second Edition.*

Tabb (John B.).

POEMS. Sq. 32mo. 4s. 6d. net.

Tennyson (Frederick).

POEMS OF THE DAY AND YEAR. With a Title-page designed by PATTEN WILSON. Crown 8vo. 5s. net.

Thimm (Carl A.).

A COMPLETE BIBLIOGRAPHY OF FENCING AND DUELLING, AS PRACTISED BY ALL EUROPEAN NATIONS FROM THE MIDDLE AGES TO THE PRESENT DAY. With a Classified Index, arranged Chronologically according to Languages. Illustrated with numerous Portraits of Ancient and Modern Masters of the Art. Title-pages and Frontispieces of some of the earliest works. Portrait of the Author by WILSON STEER, and Title page designed by PATTEN WILSON. 4to. 21s. net.

Thompson (Francis)

POEMS. With Frontispiece, Title-page, and Cover Design by LAURENCE HOUSMAN. Pott 4to. 5s. net. [*Fourth Edition.*

SISTER-SONGS: An Offering to Two Sisters. With Frontispiece, Title-page, and Cover Design by LAURENCE HOUSMAN. Pott 4to. 5s. net.

Thoreau (Henry David).

POEMS OF NATURE. Selected and edited by HENRY S. SALT and FRANK B. SANBORN, with a Title-page designed by PATTEN WILSON. Fcap. 8vo. 4s. 6d. net.

Traill (H. D.).

THE BARBAROUS BRITISHERS: A Tip-top Novel. With Title and Cover Design by AUBREY BEARDSLEY. Crown 8vo, wrapper. 1s. net.

FROM CAIRO TO THE SOUDAN FRONTIER. With Cover Design by PATTEN WILSON. Crown 8vo. 5s. net.

Tynan Hinkson (Katharine)

CUCKOO SONGS. With Title-page and Cover Design by LAURENCE HOUSMAN. Fcap. 8vo. 5s. net.

MIRACLE PLAYS. OUR LORD'S COMING AND CHILDHOOD. With 6 Illustrations, Title-page, and Cover Design by PATTEN WILSON. Fcap. 8vo. 4s. 6d. net.

Walton and Cotton.

THE COMPLEAT ANGLER. Edited by RICHARD LE GALLIENNE. Illustrated by EDMUND H. NEW. Fcap. 4to, decorated cover. 15s. net.

Also to be had in thirteen 1s parts.

Watson (Rosamund Marriott).

VESPERTILIA AND OTHER POEMS. With a Title-page designed by R. ANNING BELL. Fcap 8vo. 4s. 6d. net.

A SUMMER NIGHT AND OTHER POEMS. New Edition. With a Decorative Title-page. Fcap. 8vo. 3s. net.

Watson (William).

THE FATHER OF THE FOREST AND OTHER POEMS. With New Photogravure Portrait of the Author Fcap. 8vo, buckram. 3s. 6d. net. [*Fifth Edition.*

ODES AND OTHER POEMS. Fcap. 8vo, buckram. 4s. 6d. net. [*Fourth Edition.*

Watson (William)—*continued.*

THE ELOPING ANGELS: A Caprice Square 16mo, buckram. 3s. 6d. net. [*Second Edition.*

EXCURSIONS IN CRITICISM : being some Prose Recreations of a Rhymer. Crown 8vo, buckram. 5s. ret. [*Second Edition.*

THE PRINCE'S QUEST AND OTHER POEMS. With a Bibliographical Note added. Fcap. 8vo, buckram. 4s. 6d. net. [*Third Edition.*

THE PURPLE EAST : A Series of Sonnets on England's Desertion of Armenia. With a Frontispiece after G. F. WATTS, R.A. Fcap. 8vo, wrappers. 1s. net.
[*Third Edition.*

THE YEAR OF SHAME. With an Introduction by the BISHOP OF HEREFORD. Fcap. 8vo. 2s. 6d. net. [*Second Edition.*

Watt (Francis).

THE LAW'S LUMBER ROOM. Fcap. 8vo. 3s. 6d. net.
[*Second Edition.*

Watts-Dunton (Theodore).

POEMS. Crown 8vo. 5s. net.
[*In preparation.*

There will also be an *Edition de Luxe* of this volume printed at the Kelmscott Press.

Wenzell (A. B.)

IN VANITY FAIR. 70 Drawings. Oblong folio. 15s. net.

Wharton (H. T.)

SAPPHO. Memoir, Text, Selected Renderings, and a Literal Translation by HENRY THORNTON WHARTON. With 3 Illustrations in Photogravure, and a Cover designed by AUBREY BEAROSLEY. Fcap. 8vo. 7s. 6d. net. [*Third Edition.*

THE YELLOW BOOK

An Illustrated Quarterly.

Pott 4to. 5s. net.

I. April 1894, 272 pp., 15 Illustrations. [*Out of print.*

II. July 1894, 364 pp., 23 Illustrations.

III. October 1894, 280 pp., 15 Illustrations.

IV. January 1895, 285 pp., 16 Illustrations.

V. April 1895, 317 pp., 14 Illustrations.

VI. July 1895, 335 pp., 16 Illustrations.

VII. October 1895, 320 pp., 20 Illustrations.

VIII. January 1896, 406 pp., 26 Illustrations.

IX. April 1896, 256 pp., 17 Illustrations.

X. July 1896, 340 pp., 13 Illustrations.

XI. October 1896, 342 pp., 12 Illustrations.

XII. January 1897, 350 pp., 14 Illustrations.